CH00525930

ALSO BY

Viola Di Grado

70% Acrylic 30% Wool

HOLLOW HEART

Viola Di Grado

HOLLOW HEART

*Translated from the Italian
by Antony Shugaar*

Europa
editions

Europa Editions
214 West 29th Street
New York, N.Y. 10001
www.europaeditions.com
info@europaeditions.com

Translation by Antony Shugaar
Original title: *Cuore cavo*
Translation copyright © 2015 by Europa Editions

Library of Congress Cataloging in Publication Data is available
ISBN 978-1-60945-271-1

Di Grado, Viola
Hollow Heart

Book design by Emanuele Ragnisco
www.mekkanografici.com

Cover image © Atsuo Sakazume

Prepress by Grafica Punto Print – Rome

Printed in the USA

"O unknown Nothing! O unknown Nothing!
In truth the soul can have no better vision in this life
than to see its own nothing and to stay in its prison."
—ANGELA OF FOLIGNO

HOLLOW HEART

2011

I n 2011 the world ended: I killed myself.
On July 23, at 3:29 in the afternoon, my death set out from Catania. Its epicenter was my thin, supine body, my three hundred grams of human heart, my small breasts, my puffy eyes, my brain clubbed senseless, the wrist of my right arm draped over the edge of the tub, the other wrist submerged in a grim mojito of mint bubble bath and blood.

On July 23, in the full heat of summer, down the dusty steps of my apartment building, oozing downward insidiously like oily, boiling veins of asphalt, my death propagated from Via Crispi 21 through all the neighboring streets, to the cathedral with its pigeons and shorts-clad tourists, to the Amenano River, which reeks of carrion, and then vanished underground. From my central nervous system to the streets of the city center, from cold to hot, a perfect breakdown from which there is no return. Down into the black heart of the lava stone, from the Roman aqueduct to the dirt paths of the Parco Gioeni, overgrown with weeds and littered with empty beer cans, to the scalding steps of the Church of the Santissima Trinità, to the dingy gray faces of saints Peter and Paul outside the Church of Sant'Agata al Borgo. From there it shot off to the narrow sidewalks of the Scogliera, a scream in the depths of the sea, a puff of air in the seagulls' lungs. Amidst the noise of the beaches, the sweat, the wafting clouds of deodorant and suntan lotion. Geometric under the spray of the shower, brutal down in the drains, down among the cigarette butts, inside used condoms, swirling down, martyred, into the sewers, down into the darkness and shit, tangled up in hair and the tails of passing rats. After four hours my body temperature plunged, especially that of my internal organs.

First the brain.

Then the liver.

Then the epidermis.

Then the Ionian Sea: it hardened like a fist.

At that point my death once again took wing. It flew all the way up to Mount Etna, darting among the pines of Linguaglossa, furious as an enamorment, secret as a virus. From the hollowed-out branches of my vascular system to the withered branches of the birch trees, from my long dark hair to the crowns of the maple trees, made unkempt by the muggy heat, from the dark expanses of my collapsed nerves to the expanses of sunbaked fields, off to the west, flickering for an instant as if being defibrillated and then falling still forever. Lightning-quick, wet, tangled up in the roots of every blue-green holm oak, in the Bosco Chiuso, inside every unripe acorn, all the way down into the parched soil and then up and away again. Up to an elevation of three thousand feet, black with the oak trees, tiny with the ants. Up and still farther up, all the way to the top, a fire running the wrong way round, from sky to crater. The incubation lasted two days and then, at dawn on July 25, the volcano's southeast crater suddenly erupted. Lava sloughed down the eastern slope until seven o'clock that evening. A fountain of savage blood no longer hemmed in by veins.

At that point, a powerful wind sprang up and drove the ash toward the Ionian Sea. Looking up at the sky the people of Catania were astonished by a hard black rain. Something was broken, something was now beyond repair. They all turned their burning eyes back to earth; no one recognized me. They all took shelter in their homes, surrounded by their knick-knacks and their little loves. The ash is gone, the sun has set, the lava has hardened down the length of the long arms of dark earth surrounding the volcano. For two hours, the sky remained gray, grainy, soaked in red like a used gauze dressing. A light breeze began to blow like a solace, and my death, solitary and profound, left the island.

Since that day, it has silently infected the rest of the planet, slow as smog, solemn as a void, private as a prayer, quickly becoming one of the most urgent environmental phenomena, and one of the most invisible.

Things seem the same, but the substance has drained out of them: the Ionian Sea is no longer cold and it no longer wets my skin, the ancient rock lining the Cavagrande River isn't hard enough to hinder my passage, and if I swim I can propel myself all the way into the gray uterus of the stone. Things seem the same, but the feelings have drained out of them: when I was little, the jelly that fell on the breakfast table stuck to my arms, the dust on the floor clung to the bottoms of my feet. But now everything keeps to itself.

Things seem the same, but they've lost their voice: when I was alive, if I held my fingers out toward the fire, the heat told the pain to my nerves, but now every flame has fallen mute.

In 1958, two scientists, Santini and Dell'Erba, studied the spread of rigor mortis through the body. But until now no one had ever thought to consider its geographic diffusion: how could I help but feel misunderstood? The rigor mortis of planet Earth started with my heart: not only was it the first organ in my body to stop, it was also the first to harden. Two hours after my death, while I was still in the tub, its cavities began to tighten in on themselves, and its walls thickened as if to brace themselves against this one last disappointment. Then came time for my eyelids and all the muscles of my gaunt face. Then for the muscles of my head and neck, my upper body, my belly, my slightly bowed legs, my feet. Twelve hours later, I was completely rigid. Then came time for the rest of the planet.

My name is Dorotea Giglio.

I've always been pale: as a little girl, as a grown-up, as a corpse. My hair is brown and so are my eyes, that should help you to remember me. My face is gaunt and my body is as sharp and angular as that of a young girl from the third world, just right for stirring pity in photos posted on social media. My eyes have taut, downturned eyelids, like the wings of a wounded bird in a power dive, a bird that can no longer migrate. My eyes have always been best when they're shut, like twin Pandora's boxes. Lorenzo used to watch me sleep; I always thought it was a sign of love. Then it dawned on me that I was just prettier that way. My eyes—I don't know whether it was my mother or Aunt Clara who closed them. I have freckles, like a connect-the-dots game where you make a picture, but in my case I remain invisible. My mother was thoughtful or lazy enough not to rent out my room, so I still live with her, even if she lives alone.

On the morning of July 23, 2011, I was twenty-five years old.

I was about to graduate with a degree in biology, I was taking my last five classes. I'd been working in a stationery shop near my home since I was twenty-one, and I'd been studying violin with a private tutor. For two years, I'd been taking Imipramine-based antidepressants, which made me a good daughter and a dedicated fan of TV shows like *Friends* and *The O.C.* I was always sleepy and I was calm and well mannered, with a heart that beat too fast and legs that moved too slow. My mouth was often dry; other times it refused to speak. Sometimes, at night, my pupils were too big or too small in the mirror. Now and then, lying in bed, I'd start shaking. It was all too easy for me to match shivers to memories. My own memories, or those my mother had infected me with.

Memories of Lorenzo who broke up with me via text message or of Aunt Lidia who left this world, swallowed up by water, her pockets filled with stones. Both these abandonments occurred on beautiful days in late April, in almost summery settings, with yellow sunlight and buzzing insects, with a neon-blue sky and agave plants striking coquettish poses.

Lorenzo had dumped me in seven hundred characters, the maximum length allowed for a text message before the double rate kicks in; I was sitting on the patio glider outside Aunt Clara's beach house at Costa Saracena, studying. Lidia, on the other hand, left the world without a word sixteen years before I was born. Then there was my father's abandonment: he too had left me, but at the time I was sightless and incomplete and still attached to my mother's placenta.

None of those memories belonged to me entirely, not even the ones I'd actually experienced. Having a single body forced me to coexist with all my experiences, to keep them hot in my brain, stitched to my nerves. They were always ready to visit mayhem on the happy moments I spent with Lorenzo. It would be an instant, the popping of a balloon during a party. My knees would give way and I'd fall to the carpet in the living room screaming, my hands over my eyes. My mother would step past me in stiletto heels, Lorenzo would help me to my feet.

On the morning of January 30, 2009, the day of my twenty-third birthday, coming out of my comparative anatomy class, I found Lorenzo waiting for me in his car. He'd made an appointment with a wrinkly old psychiatrist with green eyes and a fancy office in Piazza Verga, across from the courts building. There was a potted cactus in the waiting room, and a girl in a red tracksuit sitting next to me reading her horoscope in a women's magazine. Her hair was so thin that all the weirdness of the human skull was fully visible; silence reigned except for the muttering of the air conditioner. Lorenzo was talking to me, using words like "tranquility" and "calm" and "quality of life," hospice words that are good for only one thing: persuading an old person to pass away slowly in an unfamiliar bed after hours and hours playing cards with strangers. Then it was our turn. And that's when the psychopharmaceuticals enter the stage to scrub everything clean, disinfect, and leave me as tidy and breakable as a glass-front buffet.

I'd fall asleep all the time and everywhere, during my molecular biology class or on the bus, and I'd get off at random stops, in Gravina or on Via Etnea, in front of the Villa Bellini. I'd go in, wander down the shadowy walkways like a panicky animal, eyes downcast, greasy hair hanging over my eyes. Or else I'd sit down and rest on the white stone rim of the Fountain of the Swans.

That's what they still call it, the Fountain of the Swans, but the swans were killed by vandals. In March 1983 the first one vanished. In March 1984, three more. They were found a few yards away, their throats ripped open by dogs. Then two more, and two more after that, impaled on the spikes of the gate on Piazza Roma. The last swan was the loveliest of them all, I still remember it. I was fourteen years old when it would sail around the empty basin, not looking for anyone. It would stop in the center. It refused to approach my outstretched hand when I'd try to feed it my sandwich, on my way home from school. In May 2000 it was found with its throat cut.

The swans were replaced with large black ducks, raggedy and slow-witted, and then by depressing bronze herons. The basin is full of dry leaves, and gangs of thuggish girls hang around it and beat up other girls in front of anyone who cares to watch. People break off their walks and stand around, smiles yawning like genitalia, they set their glittering shopping bags down on the ground: first shopping, then a fistfight, then a pizza followed by a limoncello. Even the carabinieri, concealed at the corner behind long ficus leaves chipped with black, always stop to watch with feverish eyes. Sitting on the rim of the Fountain of the Swans I gradually tried to catch my breath. Not even Sleeping Beauty knows how short a distance it is from chronic fatigue to eternal sleep.

I got decent grades on my exams and I let the days pass just as they were, without the audacity to fill them with events and meaning: I imagined them as so many brown-edged holes left by a cigarette in a white sheet. I imagined plenty of other things, most of them monstrous, but the worst didn't need to be imagined; they already existed. My mother existed: she was the realest thing there was.

On July 19, 2011, the day of my anniversary with Lorenzo, even though he'd left me a year and three months earlier, I wanted to commemorate the date by sleeping for twenty-four hours. Instead I woke up at seven fifteen in the morning in a pool of piss and sweat. This happened sometimes. I was a plant in its sopping-wet dirt. A plant, though not a sunflower, which has the healthy instinct to turn toward the light. I was a plant that never moves and takes in sunshine and water until the time comes to fold humbly in on itself and die.

My mother walked into the room wearing an iron-gray slip with a cigarette in her mouth. Her legs were glistening with moisturizing cream.

"When are you going to cut all this out? It's ridiculous."

"Mama, I'm hurting."

"Oh really? You're hurting? I ought to be the one who's hurting."

"We're both hurting."

"Christ on a crutch go get washed up what are you still doing here."

The morning of July 23 it was 108 degrees out.

My mother went out at nine in the morning to take pictures of a row of withered trees on Corso Italia. She was wearing a rust-colored silk dress, black vinyl wedge shoes, and a heavy necklace of rough-cut stones. Nine days after my funeral she would hang the best picture in the living room: three trees covered with marks and patches of missing bark like old people's arms, with tiny shelves of white mushrooms sucking the nutrients out of them. Framed in light-blue plastic, the photograph would remain there for the two years that followed my death, until Aunt Clara took it down, leaving in its place a testamentary square of wall that was a brighter shade of white.

Aunt Clara was the pretty sister, my mother the depressed one. The eldest sister was named Lidia but she had drowned in the Cassibile River, taking all her adjectives with her. Aunt Clara was the one who dreamed at night about Lidia's swollen body emerging from the water like weather-beaten wood, her face flaccid and expressionless, her fingers soft-boiled. My mother was the one who once found herself in the street late at night, standing in front of the dumpster, barefoot and wet-cheeked, so my grandmother had to go down and get her. I'm the one who would have the nightmare where there was a concave darkness like the bottom of a jar and I was suffocating inside it. All three of us taken together were a perfect hydraulic system of trauma. I was right at the mouth of the last stretch of pipe and I didn't even know what Lidia's face looked like, but the nightmare was crystal clear and it made me wake up drenched in sweat, my heart racing like crazy.

The morning of July 23 I put on my favorite dress, the red sleeveless one. Looking in the mirror I felt like Jessica Rabbit, but every impulse of self-respect I might have had was a round-trip ticket: after a couple of seconds outbound, I returned straight home to the nuisance of being myself. I put on my black canvas polka dot shoes with little straps: I didn't like to wear them much because the tension of the thin material stretched over the tips of my toes was bound to explode into a hole before long, and I didn't want that to happen: they were my favorite shoes. I pulled my dark purple lipstick out of my makeup case, but it had melted in the heat: as soon as I opened it the creamy mass broke into two soft, greasy sections and the top part fell into the sink. I tried to use the broken stump that was still attached to the base but it was too short. So I dabbed my fingertip into the gooey mess in the sink and smeared it onto my lips. I succeeded in applying it, to an extent. I picked up the eyeliner, but it too was melted; I drew rings around my eyes similar to the bruise you get when someone punches you.

I left the apartment.

The bald lawyer who lives on the fifth floor was walking ahead of me and he held the street door open with a smile. As soon as I drew close to the slit of the half-open door, the muggy air and the sunlight and a slow scent of sunbaked flowers inundated my face. The muggy air and the sunlight and the flowers still had meaning, and I was tempted to press it to my heart, but I did not.

Catania in the summer: scalding, oozing, an open wound. Constant car horns, mangy dogs, people squinting and sandals made of eco leather. Humid, unbreathable air. The heat was a dumpster full of smells, old beer and urine, gasoline, deodorants going past, and the aforementioned flowers: red and purple blooms at the corner of the sidewalk, clutching the shrouds of their already-dried petals. I crossed the street and somebody nearly ran me over: a guy wearing a white Lacoste polo shirt and Ray-Bans leaned out the window and yelled at me to go fuck myself. His girlfriend had her feet up on the dashboard and was applying pink polish to her toenails.

At the supermarket across the street I bought red plastic plates, red forks, red party cups, a bottle of cheap spumante, a frozen paella, and a bag of single-blade disposable razors.

There was a two-for-one sale, but I thought one death would be enough for me.

Sitting on an upside-down fruit crate outside the supermarket, a corpulent African woman wearing red lipstick and a long white mesh dress was clapping her large hands to the beat of something that didn't exist for me. Hanging from her neck was a sign: I'M HAPPY, PLEASE HELP ME.

I invited two girlfriends of mine to lunch: Gaia and Flavia, a pair of well-mannered young women with a sad talent for settling, which they called "being realistic." I set the table with the red Christmas tablecloth covered with reindeer. At the right-hand corner was an old wine stain. I lit a white candle at the center of the table. I filled the bathtub upstairs. I placed the razor next to the tub.

The first to arrive was Gaia; she had a fashionable new asymmetrical haircut and a freshly ironed pink blouse. She did a lot of smiling. We sat down on the sofa together and she told me about a fight with Paolo, her boyfriend: they'd disagreed about the frames of his new glasses. Then Flavia got there. She brought me the birthday present that they'd been meaning to give me for the last six months: a shiny navy-blue-and-azure knee-length dress with a sixties harlequin pattern. I thanked them very much; I did a lot of smiling. We ate the paella, I tore every bite into little pieces with my teeth and sent it safe and sound down my esophagus. All the windows and even the door had been opened in an attempt to let in some air, but there wasn't so much as a breeze, and every time someone climbed the apartment building's stairs the enormous sound of footsteps reached us from the landing. Sitting there at the table, with the candle almost melted, each of us waited with bated breath for the stream of air from the fan to hit us.

"Dorotea?"

"What?"

"Why is this candle here, anyway? In the morning, with all this heat?"

" . . . "

"Dorotea, did you hear me?"

"Yes. Sorry, girls, I have a splitting headache."

"Take an aspirin, do you have one? I might have some Tylenol in my bag, you want me to look?"

"No, no, thanks, I'm super tired too, I think I'll just take a nap."

"It's still because of those pills, isn't it? Why do you keep taking them?"

"No, they don't have anything to do with it. I just want to get some sleep."

They left, promising that we'd go to the movies the next day and see *Paranormal Activity 3*. Flavia's boyfriend, Moreno, preferred going to the second show so he could study until late. I closed the door behind them. I turned on the TV; they were showing an American series with vampires or ghosts or young couples in love, it wasn't clear yet. As I climbed the stairs to the second story of our apartment, canned laughter accompanied me: so it was supposed to be funny. What was it called? Who produced it, who conceived it? Who has laughed or wept or hated life while watching each episode? I would never know the answers to these questions. I'd never get any kind of answer at all, ever again. Before slipping into the chilly water I hung up the dress in my wardrobe. It would have gone perfectly with those light-blue ballet flats, the velvet ones with the bows.

It was 3:20 in the afternoon and my mother was at Aunt Clara's, celebrating. Aunt Clara had just gotten a promotion at the textbook publisher where she worked; that's why—as I slipped into the tub—crystal glasses were being raised on a terrace filled with carefully tended plants in Costa Saracena. I picked up the razor. I closed my eyes.

I thought of the ascomycete. That fungus whose spores land on an insect and then dig into it. The fungus grows inside it, slowly destroying the insect's organs, until the insect becomes an empty sarcophagus. Finally, the mushroom erupts, enormous, disintegrating in an instant the body that by now belongs to it alone. It was a story Lorenzo had told me: at the time he was taking his doctorate in entomology. I listened with interest: at the time I was alive. We were sitting on the glider at Aunt Clara's beach house, where we always spent hours and hours in the summer. We were wearing swimsuits; mine was a strawberry-colored bikini. The heat was atrocious, my mother was dressed in white, watering plants, and she seemed like a woman dressed in white watering plants. For the past few months she'd been doing much better than usual, and she would persist in that radiant normality until my death. On the balcony of the house next door a German shepherd was sleeping, wearing an orthopedic collar. My water-puckered fingers clutched the plastic razor, my eyes focused on the blue of my veins, I sliced my right wrist: error.

I tried again: error.

Nausea flooded my throat.

On the third try I felt a profound shock surge up from beneath the skin, sweeping through the entire organism, crying out for a full range of the body's ambulances. The blood was warm. The blood wasn't strange. I moved on to the left wrist. When the mushroom is about to split the insect open, the insect goes racing crazily up a tree, and then it suddenly shatters into pieces. The razor fell to the white tiles. Downstairs, on TV, there was a burst of canned laughter.

I still wonder why the insect starts running.

What is it trying to reach up there, at all costs? What is this thing, so strong and so punctual that every invaded insect feels it, always in the same instant, the moment before dying? Why did this thing not exist until just a second before, and why does it suddenly announce its existence in such an absolute manner? And who is it, inside the insect, that senses the arrival of the final moment? Is it the insect, what little remains of it, or is it the fungus?

I don't know why I would be thinking of insects just before shuffling off.

If only they too—from the tiny flies to the *Nicrophorus humator*, terrifying stowaways in my corpse—would be still for a second and think of me in the pitch-darkness of my flesh, perhaps they'd rethink their destructive campaign and finally stop making me die.

Four years have passed since my death.

The sky is still blue and people still live in houses. They hire gardeners to look after their yards and partners to look after their loneliness. They put moisturizing lotion on their skin and they put their hearts at rest. They watch movies on TV with Jennifer Aniston or Sandra Bullock, and they find them attractive. When spring comes, they put their overcoats in special cellophane bags and return them to their closets, they take advantage of the cafés with outdoor tables in the cathedral square to chat with their friends, and they inevitably gape in surprise at how the days have grown longer. Global warming and the hole in the ozone layer haven't yet progressed from theory to outright apocalypse, and the cellophane garment bags for overcoats still say "an indispensable aid to ensure that your garments are safe from insects."

My name is Dorotea Giglio and I'm full of flies. However much civilization might have trained you to be frightened of people like me, no one's more scared than I am.

After my adolescence, there was a small chunk of adult life that I made exceedingly poor use of, followed immediately by livor mortis: two hours after my death I was red from head to toe. Then came rigor mortis, and by this point my eyes could be pulled open only from outside, like a doll's. Then autolysis, or self-digestion. My cells self-destructed, one by one, until I was completely purified within: the final and ultimate examination of conscience.

Putrefaction was the most depressing part. That's when the insects came along. The first-string squad, then the second-string, and the third: that's what they call them, squads, and they always win, because I'm no longer an opponent, just a playing field. Last came the fourth-string squad. Like the others they went into me and they stayed a good long time: I am a first-class hotel, very discreet, and I cost nothing. Five months after passing away I was already popular: my skin filled up with black butterflies, whores with fast mouths and long outspread wings. They tore at my tissues as if they were so much wallpaper, until the terrible wall of my bones emerged.

And we're not done yet.

Then *Dermestes lardarius* showed up, followed by the *Nicrophorus humator*. Slimy little vandals, with long dark legs that never seem to stand still. It's their fault that my skin kept coming apart like party streamers, soft and red. What frightful festivities! All of nature was on the guest list. The cockroaches undid my ligaments, the *Galasa cuprealis* eagerly chowed down at the buffet table of my withered tendons. The beetles, unscrupulous tourists that they are, have been permanent guests in my arms—unbuttoned like antique gloves on my bare muscles—since 2012. Very soon, bleached clean of all signs of life, my skeleton will be as spotless and reassuring as sheets drying under the sunny skies of detergent commercials. Very soon, I'll be gone.

Today is March 1, 2015.

Aboveground, spring has already arrived, but underground a black ooze is spreading, littered with dissolved scraps of my flesh and the rags of the sky-blue linen dress in which I was buried. In the Parco Falcone, surrounded by plane trees and palm trees and empty beer cans, the first petunias have bloomed. They burst out of the soil, without shyness, everywhere. At the foot of the red, orange, and blue jungle gym with the little metal slide. Under the empty benches. Under the chairs where old men play cards. Flowers spring up everywhere: the sun bestows its rays equitably upon them all; none are outsiders. There's plenty of sunlight for all of them, and all of them will grow. My body, at the Catania city cemetery, tucked away where the sky can't see it, dreams of that same growth and that same consideration on the part of the sun. It dreams of it the same way that it dreamed with me of becoming an astronaut when I was a little girl. It dreams of it but nature is Giuliana, the little elementary-school bully: even now that I'm a skeleton like all the other skeletons, I'm an outsider. Even now, with my empty eye sockets, the little fair-haired fifth-grade boy can still tell me I look like a whipped puppy. Even now, when all I have under my eyes is a jigsaw puzzle of deteriorating tissues, out on the playground the whole class still calls me "wicked witch" because of the circles under my eyes. Inside the coffin, I suffer as if there were still some remedy for my loneliness. As if my father might come back any minute now to tuck in what little skin remains to me.

In the meantime, the spring continues.

Daisies pop up over my dying body. To be exact, a good long way above it. There's a considerable distance between us. The flowers live at an elevation I can no longer hope to attain: I'm no longer at their level, and there's nothing I can do about it. Nature establishes a very rigid hierarchy. Now self-esteem is a matter of fertilizer: I no longer have any need for compliments and fulfilling relationships, nor do I care about achieving my goals. No matter what I do, the flowers will always stand head and shoulders above me.

People will see them and sometimes they'll decide to pick them and take them home. As for me, there's no longer any part of me that people can pick: they can't even pick up on my witticisms and my ideas, since no one ever hears them anymore. The sun is friends with everyone, like a politician, but it can't do anything for me now. My body is stretched out like a pan-handler's imploring hand: it begs for light or vitamin D, but it never gets anything at all.

In the Catania cemetery, a boxwood hedge—with its twisted trunk, its greenish bark—has taken root a few earthen floors above me and soon it will be closer to the sky, and to heaven, than I'll ever be. My soul, in fact, never reached its destination, the afterlife that all religions count on. My soul stayed right here, like a foul residue stuck to the bottom of the pan. My soul is me.

It sounds saccharine or, even worse, New-Agey, but there's nothing I can do about it, that's my identity. It's my identity, but really it's closer to an atmospheric phenomenon of some sort.

Censored by my invisibility, I watch the others go on living. I recognize them, I understand them, I have plenty of words for them, but they can no longer see me. I'm invisible: the matter I'm made of is indecent, it demands secrecy. I'm invisible: I can no longer depress anyone with my depression, I can't influence with my opinions, I can't stir pity. I'm invisible: my body is taboo. I'm invisible, but it's all a terrible misunderstanding.

Ladies and gentlemen, the sickness has passed: the heart has stopped, and with it all the other symptoms. Ladies and gentlemen, leave a contribution in flowers by my headstone corresponding to your grief. Now you can no longer use me or hurt me: now the worms are having their turn. You can't tread on me either: the tree roots will reach me first. Ladies and gentlemen, don't leave: my death, underground, goes on and on and on.

1986

My mother created me at age twenty-six, on a rainy day, in a dark kitchen with microwaves and pot holders shaped like animals. She had long legs and long lips and a husky voice. The kitchen belonged to a former classmate from college. And so did the sperm.

It was a mistake. It was a hole in the condom.

I don't know what his name was and I don't know what color hair he had. I don't know what his eyes looked like or his favorite movies. I don't know his shoe size or the words he used most frequently. I don't know if he has a scuba-diving certification or a criminal record or one of those good-natured dogs with the smashed-in face that are so popular these days. I don't know if he's lost all his hair or if he's lost all hope. I don't know if he ever got married or what kind of work he does, whether he smokes, if he plays computer games, if he likes spicy food, if he has an electric toothbrush, a pink shirt in his dresser drawer that he never wears, a picture of someone in his wallet, or a subscription to a magazine he doesn't read. I don't know if he has holes in his socks, a sweet tooth, a gift for telling jokes, whether he wakes up early, drinks coffee, whether he laughs with his mouth shut or open so wide that you can see his gums, I don't know what he wears around the house or what he reads at night before falling asleep, I don't know whether he reads and I don't even know if he sleeps, I don't know whether he talks a little or a lot, I don't even know if he talks at all, I don't know if he's mute, I don't know if he's alive.

I don't know any of these things and I almost never want to know them.

They weren't even dating; they didn't know each other's last names. They just met at a party at the house of a mutual acquaintance, they'd talked about school and about what they were doing: he still wasn't doing anything at all. Then back to his place, that same night. And in the weeks that followed, a couple of movies and a drink at a bar in Piazza Teatro Massimo. Then that was it. After he got the news, a month later, she never heard from him again. But she swore to me that he came to celebrate my third birthday, that he was there, he was there. Then gone forever.

This is all I know and I often tell myself that it's all I need to know, and I almost always believe it. My mother never told me anything else about him, except that she certainly didn't need some asshole at her side to raise me. She never answered my questions about him, and before long I started keeping those questions to myself. After a while I had fewer and fewer of them. They withered from lack of sunlight.

My mother had lips as long as asps and her name was Greta; I got to know her with the masks of her camera lenses between us. After my birth she rented an apartment with a cellar storage area. She immediately turned the little cellar space into a darkroom, and the rest of the apartment into a dark apartment. We used electricity only sparingly because we had so little money, and we used our faces to smile only sparingly because happiness wasn't something we did well.

I was born by natural childbirth in a bathtub and I died of unnatural death in the same place. I grew up surrounded by old furniture that reeked of stale wood, the furniture of grandparents I'd never seen. In the living room there was a large mirror with gilt edges, and the reflections in it were opaque and deformed, gray and split in half by a crack. Whenever I looked at myself I'd decide to be either the one on the right or, other times, the one on the left. The windows were always open and the curtains twisted and tangled, the parquet floor was covered with crushed dry leaves that came rustling in from the outside world and didn't know how to get back out to it.

Four beechwood chairs in the dining room: two empty ones next to the table, the other two relegated to the corners. On the chair in the left-hand corner sat a mangy teddy bear missing its right eye that had belonged to Lidia when she was a girl. On the chair in the opposite corner was the empty cage that once held two hamsters I'd been given for my fifth birthday, but after a week the boy hamster had gnawed the girl hamster's legs off: we didn't find her mutilated body until she was dead, and my mother threw the killer hamster into the toilet as a punishment, but he kept coming back up, bug-eyed, so she'd had to flush five times. A dining room table in black walnut, and on it camera lenses and empty cigarette packs and a black-and-white photograph torn into pieces so small that it was impossible to say what they depicted. Overhead, a fifties crystal chandelier, solid and drab as a dog's teeth, and all around it long gums of dampness spreading out across the whole ceiling. Very little daylight came in, and when it did it soon regretted it. Like a moth, it wanted to return outside but didn't know how. Like a moth, it ran blindly into things, misunderstood them, feared them.

And dust everywhere. Between the doorjambs. Even on the lacquered side table by the front door, around the broken wing of the small porcelain phoenix that Aunt Clara brought back from her first honeymoon in China. Dust engulfing the legs of the chairs in the dining room, both the empty ones and the ones in the corner. Dust on the raised arm of the teddy bear and in the unstitched hole where his missing eye had once been.

Even the television was covered with dust. And if you moved a piece of furniture you were blinded by a toxic cloud of fine gray grit. Thick, grainy dust. An entire fortress of dust under my bed, even inside the shoebox where I kept my diary.

Dust on my shelves between one book and the next. Dust that went on to spawn more dust, and that in my death fermented, expanded, monstrified. Dust that developed legs and arms, strings of gray muscle that now extend over my bed and my windowsill, filling the red mug full of pens, and the crack between my bathroom door and the wall. They even fill your eyes if you look at any object close up. They cling to your fingertips if you touch the green alarm clock, the nightstand, the locked armoire, or the sink, or the bathtub. Now the sofa in front of the TV is wrapped in a clear plastic slipcover and on it the dust rests peacefully, like the remains of a tattered beast. Indestructible dust, fairy dust, from dust we are born and to dust we shall return.

But there was never a spider to be seen. No doubt there were plenty. Hidden under the sofas, behind the dark-blue curtains, concealed in the cracks in the walls. But faced with all that dust, they felt challenged. They sensed that their construction work would be somehow excessive, a pointless effort. They understood that the apartment itself was one huge spiderweb made up of many smaller ones, and they were afraid. My mother had already been caught in it. My mother was also the black widow. I was never anyone at all.

We never saw the cockroaches either.

Nor the ants.

But I knew they were there, somewhere. I sensed their presence. Hidden in the darkness of the doorjambs, lurking in the pasta and medicine drawers, in the kitchen. Lined up in the folds in things, in the dark recesses between one object and another. Along the black outline of the coffeemaker, in the bottoms of cups that were never used, of espresso pots whose lids were never lifted.

They were there, lying in wait, spiders, ants, and cockroaches. They waited, motionless, in their hiding places. After my death, they all came out into the open.

1990

M y mother did children's fashion photography.
This was before little girls started dressing like
grown women affected by dwarfism. In those days
you wouldn't see five-year-old girls going around dressed in
sand-colored trench coats and mini-jeans, with mini-Hogans
on their feet. With my light-blue velvet baby-doll dresses with
openwork lace collars and floral-patterned wool stockings I
was a living porcelain figurine, covered with ribbons and tat-
ting, buttons shaped like animals, red and fuchsia jackets. I
posed for her often: overalls in sugar-candy hues, cartwheel
skirts with appliqués of roses and violets, reassuring lace baby-
doll collars and patent-leather flats with straps.

She started taking pictures of me down in the cellar, outside
the darkroom door. In the only interview she was ever asked to
give, she said: "I want to reduce as much as possible the distance between where a picture is conceived and where it comes
into the world. It's like giving birth at home. That's what I did
with Dorotea."

"And who do you use for models?"

"No one but her, my daughter, Dorotea. But I don't do
what Arturo Ghergo did, when he photographed his daughter
completely naked, so you could see every inch of her . . . Quite
the opposite, you see so little of Dorotea . . . I want to make
her disappear entirely."

Down in the cellar there was only enough room for her and
me, me with my fingers clutching the door handle. The door

was made of dark walnut, and it was very old, stripped bare around the doorjamb. A bare lightbulb hanging from the ceiling, and the spotlights that my mother put there. That tiny space gave us a sense of peace.

She used low light and long exposure times. She would dodge the beam of the spotlight with her long fingers loaded with costume jewelry, faux stones in red, green, and yellow. In the pictures I was a dark, abstract presence, my facial features impossible to recognize. My face blended into the peeling wall to the right of the door, under the small high window with horizontal grating. I started from me and turned into the wall.

Outside the hours passed, the postman came, Aunt Clara called us for lunch and my mother hushed her. The eight o'clock news broadcast began on the neighbors' television sets, along with the sound of barking on the balconies. The cats began to brawl. My pale legs were rivers that flowed into the wall, and so were my arms.

In the evening, I'd leaf through *The Encyclopedia of Biology*, whose volumes I kept on a shelf over the TV. At night, my nightmare of being trapped in the jar would wake me up: me in the darkness, me gasping for air. I'd go into my mother's bedroom and she'd take me back to my bed or sometimes she'd just let me sleep with her. She never told me a nice bedtime story, because we already had too many stories inside us, and because bedtime was never going to be nice.

We spent both our summer and Christmas holidays in Trecastagni.

It was the house where my mother grew up with her sisters. It was the emptiest house I'd ever seen. My grandparents had left it to Clara, then they'd died but she hadn't wanted it; she'd married a lawyer with two gold teeth and they'd moved to the beach. My mother had taken all the furniture and put it in our apartment. The house in Trecastagni had been left with nothing but a table and a dowry of spiderwebs covering the ceiling, including the hanging lamps, and even the dead lightbulbs.

There was plenty of silence and the pale yellow wall of the living room had four nail holes from nails that were no longer there. There was my mother who one night in early September was drinking limoncello with Aunt Clara in the courtyard, talking about an old romantic movie they'd just watched. Between my mother and my aunt stood an empty chair upon which twenty-five leaves and sixteen pine needles had accumulated over the years. There was also the broken-off trunk of a pine tree on which a black cat often slept, and a small twisted olive tree. There was me, sitting on the terra-cotta tile floor, leafing through the encyclopedia of biology that Aunt Clara had given me for Christmas, hot off the press from the publishing house where she worked. In the encyclopedia there were bacteria and insects and the human body. There was fog in the sky and red lipstick on all three of our mouths. There was a bedroom with the door locked but from the window you could see inside: three beds pushed together with no room between them.

Lidia the Other Sister died at age twenty-one during an excursion to the country.

Everyone could hear Lidia crying in the shower. It happened every morning. Little by little, her sobs became background noise, like traffic.

Lidia had left the university, where she'd been studying ancient Greek. Now she locked herself in her room for hours at a time, doing what, no one knew. My mother would knock and knock and knock at the door. Before that, on the nights my grandmother was just too depressed and had slept all day, while Clara was out with some boy, Greta and Lidia would talk for hours. They had a wonderful relationship, Aunt Clara told me so one day when we were swimming in the pool at Costa Saracena. They went clothes shopping together and sat under the pine tree singing cartoon theme songs. Now the pine tree has been uprooted by a cyclone, but the pine needles are still there on the empty chair.

That morning Aunt Clara was sixteen years old and had stayed home with her father. They both had the flu. It was the twenty-eighth of April and it was already hot out. My grandmother Dorotea had driven all the way out to Cavagrande, where two old girlfriends from high school were waiting for her, along with lakes as still as glass. It was a perfect day for swimming. The rocky cliffs arched up over deep gorges, full of crabs and little black fish. My grandmother stretched out next to her girlfriends. I don't know what my grandmother looks like because I've never met her. No one was there. The sun was hidden behind long gray clouds. Greta and Lidia walked off. The sounds of the wind and the water could be heard. Lidia suggested they play hide-and-seek.

"Why are you putting rocks in your pockets?"

"Because I'm collecting them."

In the pictures that my mother took of me, my body was no longer a box, it was just water. My dark hair blended into the texture of the wall, the balloon dress cut through the air like a wave. I posed with my back to the wall.

I never stopped disappearing, never stopped emerging from myself as if from a swimming pool. The lens was the mouth of a dangerous, ravening beast: the maw of the diaphragm, gaping wide, cut away my contours like so much bread crust. They created in the core of matter a secret alcove of muscles and plaster. The lens was the anxious mouth of a shark.

Afterward, in the darkroom, I watched my image being born out of the reddish darkness of the chemical bath.

The pictures were rejected by *Lulù Bimbi*. Instead they published ordinary pictures of little girls with cheeks where their cheeks should be and arms where their arms should be.

Aunt Clara wouldn't speak to us for a month. She would come to lunch, she would cook, she would say over and over: "But if it goes on like this, how will you pay your rent? You can't just rely on the money I give you."

Until finally my mother gave in. She embraced with disgust the aesthetic compromises that the market demanded. She started photographing me outdoors, not far from our building, in the little piazza off Largo Pascoli: it was summer, I was sweating in the heavy cotton of my bonbon box of an outfit, decorated with embroidered cherries and brightly colored ribbons. The florist there had gone to high school with my mother, and he gave her permission to take my picture surrounded by his flowers. The air reeked of gasoline, instead of carrying the magical scent of old wood in the cellar room.

It's been four years since my death. I drown in the ooze like a broken ship without a captain. Again today, empty tubes of toothpaste will be tossed out, and millions of obedient muscles will activate smiles.

1991

Every Christmas and every summer we'd go to the house in Trecastagni: me, my mother, and sometimes Aunt Clara, who in the meantime had begun proceedings for her divorce. I would do my holiday homework sitting at the kitchen table. My mother would wander around taking pictures and come home with groceries; the times that Aunt Clara came with us she'd work at her typewriter. We socialized with my mother's childhood friends, with their husbands and their children and their dogs. Every day I asked her to show me the pictures of Lidia that were locked in a drawer in the bedroom that was itself under lock and key, but she would always move on to another topic or another room. I'd beg her every night, when she went to bed: "Please, please, open up the locked room for me," but she'd just shut her eyes and her mouth. She'd fall asleep.

At night we'd watch TV, she'd have something to drink, and she'd go to bed. Aunt Clara slept on the couch, my mother and I would sleep together in my grandparents' bed. She'd put on a nightgown. She'd close her eyes, I'd close my eyes.

She never took my picture again.

One day she opened the white envelope with my pictures and said:

"Hey, come here. Pick one."

I picked the one that showed the least of my face.

"Good."

The next day she told me that she'd sent it to my father; she said that he'd asked for it, and she never mentioned it again.

Twenty-one days later it was July 23, 1991, and we drove all the way to Costa Saracena.

The sun was baking hot, the temperature had climbed by ten degrees in just a few hours. Aunt Clara was at the beach with her new boyfriend, a skinny guy with a tattooed back. I'd just come back from the apartment house pool, and I was still in my swimsuit: a yellow bikini dotted with red cherries. My mother was out on the balcony smoking a cigarette in a gray-and-blue sarong covered with sea turtles. Sitting on the wicker lounge chair, eyes half open, legs crossed.

I saw a car go by, I saw a man from behind. A powerful, terrifying sensation swept over me.

The car vanished. The sensation didn't. That man was my father. I hadn't seen his face. And even if I had, I'd have had no way to recognize him: I didn't know what my father looked like. But *that man was my father.* A thought so powerful that it had no need for any logical tripod.

I stood there, in the middle of the walkway.

A family was heading down to the water, dragging their feet, loaded down with inflatable mattresses, water wings, and pails, their bodies glistening with sweat, yellow-and-red baseball caps on their heads. The two little boys stopped to look at me. The mother was fat and she said: "Gabriele, Giorgio, come along." She had bulging eyes and the straps of her golden swimsuit had fallen off her shoulders. I was sweating down to my chest, to my belly button, to the backs of my knees. The little boys weren't moving, the younger one had a rub-on tattoo that was half rubbed off on his left shoulder. A dragon? A skeleton?

I was sweating all the way down to my elbows, down to my fingers hardened into fists. I was sweating at the porous intersection of fingertips and palms. Only then did I see the cat.

It had been hit by a car and then moved to the side of the walkway, next to a chipped yellow beach bucket and a dented empty box of Magnum ice cream bars. Guts squished out, head facing backward, one eye torn out of its socket like a porcelain button. The dried blood was already brown, and across it marched a dotted line of ants.

There wasn't so much as a breath of wind.

The scalding asphalt, the enflamed low terra-cotta wall covered with ivy, like new skin growing over a wound: everything was far too exposed. The faces of the two little boys and their mother, motionless, calcinated by the light and the sweat, were bits of prehistoric statues, brought into the light of this moment that was not for them.

The family started moving again. They headed toward the water. I looked at my hands. Fingers. Legs. Low wall. Stomach. Cat. My knees were trembling. Should I take its body away? Bury it in my garden? Give it a funeral, recite prayers over it? At least push the protruding bone of the sternum back in with my fingers? Or, at the very least, push it away from there, from the dirty edge of that walkway, and conceal it behind a tree? I broke out in a cold sweat. Those shivers—were they the same ones I'd feel from age twenty-three on, under the blankets, with the pills in my stomach, every night? And what about me? Am I the same person?

I looked at the cat.

The cat wasn't an act of cruelty. The cat wasn't an act of cruelty and that man wasn't my father. The cat wasn't an act of cruelty and that man wasn't my father and the cat wasn't me. Aunt Clara found us together, on the low wall, an hour later.

First grade began.

Aunt Clara gave me the books I needed. Then she took me to the mall to buy notebooks, pencils, colored markers, and a pencil sharpener. I chose a light-blue backpack with an illustration of a mermaid. I really liked it. When we got home I ran, beside myself with excitement, all the way to my mother's bedroom to show her everything, but she was lying down and had a fixed stare, her cigarette motionless in her mouth. She said: "Go away, leave me alone."

I didn't like the backpack anymore.

One October morning I remember I had a canker sore behind my upper molars. I ran my tongue over the ridge of my palate as I was leaving my bedroom. The backpack was terribly heavy on my back, I was six years old, I had the taste of milk in my mouth, it was dark in the living room, and my mother was standing by the window, looking out, clutching Lidia's teddy bear to her chest.

"What are you looking at, Mama?"

"Nothing, now get going. The school bus will be here soon."

"You look sad. What happened?"

"Everything's fine. I'm just tired. Don't worry."

Outside I heard the chimes of the ice cream man, like the movie score that suggests the appropriate emotion. But inside the radio was tuned to a raspy voice: it was Radio Maria broadcasting the Mass in Latin.

Regina angelorum . . .
Regina patriarcharum . . .
Regina prophetarum . . .
Regina apostolorum . . .

"Mama, if you're tired you should go get some sleep."

"Did I ever tell you that when I was a girl I was a sleepwalker? Every night, Grandma opened the window at three in the morning. She'd set her alarm because it always happened, without fail. She'd see me in the yard, by the pine tree, standing or else sitting in the chair. She'd come get me, without waking me up. I kept it up for a while in this house too. I'd go off right there, look, where the recycling bin for glass is now. More or less until you were a year old. Your grandmother would sleep over quite often to help me take care of you."

"I don't remember it. What was I like when I was little?"

"You were clingy. You always wanted me to carry you, to hold you in my arms, like a little lapdog. If I put you down for a second you'd burst into tears. You wouldn't let me sleep. And you'd never stop looking at me, you'd look at me in this particular way, as if . . ."

She turned to look at me.

Regina martyrum . . .

Regina confessorum . . .

Regina sine labe originali concepta . . .

"Now go to school, it's late, hurry up."

"You should go to bed if you're so tired."

"Yes, you're right, but now get going."

"No. I'm going to sleep with you."

"Do as you please."

She went to bed. I lay down next to her. She turned over on her side, one hand under her right cheek. I turned over on my side, one hand under my right cheek.

Two hours later the phone rang.

"Ciao, sweetheart, it's Aunt Clara, can I talk to your mama?"

"Ciao. No, you can't, she's sleeping."

"Why didn't you go to school today?"

"I have to stay here to make sure that Mama doesn't die."

She decided to come over.

I hadn't seen her in a while. She'd dyed her hair dark red. And maybe she was a little thinner than she used to be, but it was hard to say: both she and my mother had always been very skinny. Like me. Maybe like Lidia. Maybe like my grandmother. My mother was the skinniest one. Clara was the prettiest one. I was the palest one. Lidia was the deadest one, though not always.

Clara cooked for both of us and told me about the 1992 catalog for her publishing house, about all the updated school textbooks that would be coming out in January. Even my encyclopedia of biology had been reissued in an updated edition, but she assured me that everything that was written in my encyclopedia was still true. She made a cutlet for me. She and my mother didn't talk much, like always.

"It's so yummy, Aunt Clara, it's the yummiest cutlet in the world."

She smiled. "Do you want a little more juice?"

"No, thanks, it's full of sugar: it's bad for your teeth."

"Why, what a good little girl you are!"

She smiled again. Where had she learned to do that?

Later, while they were clearing the table, I went to the bathroom, shut the door, and studied myself in the mirror. I concentrated. I lifted my cheek muscles. My cheeks tugged at my lips, and my lips uncovered my teeth. My heart raced with excitement: it was a mystery, but it worked inside of me too.

My mother went on doing second-rate photo shoots for weddings, and between jobs she'd photograph flowers that she bought from the florist on our street and scattered over the filthy rims of toilets in the public restrooms or on some dented car, or in the open mouth of a Xerox machine, or set precariously on a manhole cover.

She held a couple of shows at her friend Adriana's gallery, and I think that hardly anyone came to them, because she was angrier all the time and talked to me less and less. She never attended the parent-teacher meetings but luckily Aunt Clara gave me all the school textbooks. I met Gaia and Flavia, who copied my classwork. I quickly learned to draw on the well of myself for everything I didn't have. Like that shark in the encyclopedia of biology, *Isistius brasiliensis*, that swallows its own teeth to get the calcium it lacks.

At night my mother would read a book and drink chardonnay from the bottle. She'd fall asleep. I'd give her a kiss on the lips. But it wasn't a kiss, it was a way of sucking venom out of a snakebite.

I took in her sadness and I never spat it out. I kept it inside me, mixed with my own. My soul was infected, I had a Siamese-twin soul, it burned in my throat.

I didn't want to grow up.

I wanted to remain a little girl for the day my father would come home.

I was afraid that, when that day finally came, he'd open the door but he wouldn't recognize me. If I was too grown-up, I'd no longer be the little girl he'd seen on my third birthday, and then he wouldn't want to take me back. It would have been better to die than to become someone else. Instead I kept growing. It started inside my mouth: the gums emptied themselves of baby teeth and in their place rose teeth that were larger, more solid. The clothes got smaller and the hair got longer. The shoes started to pinch the toes. Even the facial features grew. The diameter of the waist and the tip of the nose both grew. Everything on my face that was soft and round turned hard and pointy. The desk sank lower and my bedroom grew narrower. Hair grew under the arms and between the legs. The legs grew too, they became very long and thin, and the knees as white and protruding as the eyes. My voice grew and turned darker, the fingernails grew and filled up with black. The fingers grew, the city grew, the shops changed, there was more and more smog filling our lungs, the wet patches grew on the ceiling in my bedroom, and the freckles spread across my face. On the ceiling the wet patches took the shapes of animals scratching at the walls of their cage because they want to get out but they lack the strength. My face, rather, took on the shape of my mother's.

In winter and fall and spring I came home from school on foot, alone, and I waited for her to come home with her flowers. She didn't talk to me much. In the summer she'd take me to the beach at Lido Sole and underwater I'd search for sea urchin skeletons and I had goggles on, they were so tight that it felt as though they were encapsulating my eyes like pistachio shells. Underwater there were seashells that I could turn over. Fish that I could catch. Abalone shells that I could collect and string on a piece of twine and hang around my neck. A stronger wave washed roughly over me, my mother was sunbathing on the raft with her eyes closed behind her big cat-eye sunglasses and under her large red sun hat. I swam for shore, panting, as the waves got bigger and bigger. My ears were full of wind and my nose was full of saltwater, and so was my throat, and the waves were full of white detergent bubbles and dark spongy seaweed: the signs were unequivocal, my father wouldn't be coming home.

One morning the door buzzer buzzed and I ran to the window with my heart racing, but it wasn't my father, it was the mailman. I stood there looking out until my mother appeared in her nightgown: "I'm going to do some shopping. Don't go out."

When I heard the sound of the door locking behind her I took the poppies off the windowsill. She'd told me about photographing them spread out and scattered on the curb of the sidewalk.

I drank the water from the vase.

It was disgusting. It slopped off my lips and drenched first my dress, then the red-and-blue Persian carpet. I swallowed. I vomited onto the carpet.

In the days that followed I did this again a number of times. I don't know why I was doing it. But I do know that my mother didn't notice a thing. When I'd wake up at night from the dream of the empty jar I'd go get the flowers from the windowsill. The dream would continue to obsess me for several minutes afterward: the sensation of suffocating, the curved glass around my body. Looking out at the deserted street, which was illuminated by a single streetlight that isolated the recycling bin for glass, I'd drink and then throw up. I was a stone fountain. I was the drainage canal Lidia's swollen corpse passed through at night.

My mother was sleeping a lot now. Every night, before going to sleep, I'd continued kissing her on the lips. My kiss was an antidote to cure her of her illnesses: depression, anxiety, Lidia's death, my own birth.

When I turned seven she took me to church. She'd never been religious. Everything smelled like incense. The light was bruised and humiliated, the way it is in all churches. We listened to Mass without ever looking each other in the eye. The church sold prayer cards. One card said: "Jesus is looking for a house to share with you."

My mother bought it and put it in my Tweety Bird coin purse.

Jesus is looking for a house to share with you.

I was afraid of Him. I imagined Him lurking behind doors, ready to ambush me. I imagined His body, sculpted and bloody, emerging crabwise from behind the living-room curtains. I imagined Him watching TV with us at night, crucified on the wall between the bookshelf and the bathroom door. If I was chilly, He'd offer me His winding sheet, but only because He wanted praise from my mother: "He's such a good boy, always thinking of others."

At dinner He'd multiply the fishes because my mother as usual hadn't bought anything. Every morning He'd pull the nails out of His hands and dip them in my milk, so when I drank it I'd drown, and He'd come to my rescue, His muscular arms moving with lightning speed to force the nails up out of my throat and away from my mouth. Even then my mother would say to me, as I slumped over on the floor, bloody-mouthed: "You see what a good sweet boy He is? Not like you, who are good for nothing and take up all of my time."

When she got home from the weddings she photographed she was often drunk.

She'd give me a dry little kiss and go to bed. Other times she wasn't drunk and was actually far too wide awake, and so I'd tell her a story set in Costa Saracena where we all lived on the seabed, the whole family together, including Aunt Clara and the dead grandparents, like fish. She'd pull her glass vial with the magic potion out of her drawer.

She'd gulp down her goodnight Lexotan.

Once she was asleep I'd take three drops myself: I thought that the more of it we took the sooner my underwater story would come true.

On the day of my First Communion it was very hot out.

Aunt Clara had put together a party at her beach house. The two sisters walked together, in silence, among the festively bedecked tables. They each wore a white lace dress, long and old, let out in the sleeves and the waist, and their hair was pulled back in the same style. They moved among the guests, distributing cold antipasti and even colder smiles. Their shoes were also practically identical, patent leather décolleté pumps. Also the gray makeup and round circles of rouge on their cheeks, the red lipstick, the furrowed brows. They'd always been a matched set: the tense, uneasy faces, predisposed to wrinkle even in early childhood, and the gray bug eyes, like poorly sewn buttons on a cheap jacket. The dark circles scooped out under their eyes with strange precision, like the insides of spoons, where, on days like that one, you could see sweat gleaming. The long, shiny red lips. The well-shaped nose with flaring nostrils. The fair skin. The hair bark brown, like mine.

Then the same awkward hostility toward the other: my mother manifested hers with silence, Aunt Clara with pat phrases.

The two things—silence and pat phrases—fit together perfectly: a harlequin pattern of opposite colors in which neither one ever triumphed, and neither ever took offense. There were no quarrels, no misunderstandings. There was nothing, not even feelings, just dinners and parties. The only things they'd tell each other about were Clara's nightmares and my mother's sleepwalking, which had vanished by the time I turned one, though, eliminating one topic of conversation. When they smiled at each other it was by accident, it was like the smile of someone in a coma, in the dark room of a house where the body continues to grow without being aware of it. In any case, the smile disappeared immediately, as if sucked back down under the surface.

Most of all, though, they had the same eyes. It's certainly true, but I didn't mention their most important characteristic. Their most important characteristic is that they are identical to the eyes of Lidia Who Died in the River.

I imagined them frequently, those eyes: what they were like when Lidia was alive and what they were like when the water was pouring into her lungs. Then what they were like underground. I imagined them serious and feminine like the Eye of Horus painted in the pyramids, then round and watchful like a blue Turkish evil-eye bead, then squared off and geometric like the eye in Chinese ideograms. But I'd never seen them. All the pictures are hidden in that drawer, in that room with the locked door, in the villa in Trecastagni. Once they hung in the little living room, across from the fireplace: you can see from the bare patches on the wall, a brighter yellow than the rest, and from the small holes left by the nails.

I'd never seen them, those photographs. All I knew of Lidia was the silence of her sisters: the way that, at the table, between one phrase and the next, their eyes would meet by accident and they'd fall silent. I knew that this was why my mother and my aunt never met each other's gaze: not because they hated each other, but to keep from seeing those eyes.

That morning they walked among the tables like statues of saints, with closed marble faces, slow as if being borne on a bier, covered with relics. I left the party and went down to the beach. It was deserted and silent. It was the dwelling place of the one who hadn't come to my party, and never would.

I went on growing. My breasts grew. My sadness and yearnings grew. Under my eyes the flesh sunk into dark circles that never dissipated. I grew. My mother started seeing an overweight man who was a teacher but after two months he broke up with her over the phone. She lay stretched out, clutching the receiver with one hand; I lay stretched out beside her, holding her other hand and listening to the conversation. It went on for half an hour and at a certain point she threw the lampshade at the window. The window glass was only scratched and the lampshade went rolling across the parquet floor. She was crying. The lightbulb broke and so did the external layer of my endometrium. Transparent shards on the parquet and menstruation all over my thighs. My mother took some Lexotan and fell asleep, and I went to sleep in my bedroom, leaving my first blood on her bed.

I went on growing. Everyone knows that any excessive growth within the body is a tumor. Our cells are programmed to die before exhausting their capacity for growth. Cancer cells, on the other hand, not only go on growing but invade the cells surrounding them.

As I grew, I invaded my mother. I was her illness.

I took up more and more room, I needed a bigger desk and more answers to more questions. I needed money for new clothes and bras, and for medical treatment for my scoliosis. I needed to have my spine straightened at the gym and I needed the walls of my room, ruined by dampness, to be repaired.

She glared at me and started spending more and more time out of the house. I'd wait for her in her bed.

Her table and chair were covered with clothing from the market and no one ever turned off the ceiling fan. The old parquet floor in her bedroom creaked and protested like the floors of Nijō Castle in Japan, which—due to special nails and clamps installed underneath the surface—creak in imitation of a nightingale's song when you walk on them. I read that they'd been built that way to warn the samurai whenever an intruder was walking in the hallways. Sometimes at night, now that I'm dead, even my footsteps make them creak, and when that happens my mother opens her eyes, but she sees nothing.

The bills kept piling up and Aunt Clara started to worry about it. Otherwise, I didn't go out much. One night when I was thirteen, as I sat on the sofa watching *IT*, my mother handed me a pair of pajamas and my toothbrush: "Get out of here, come back tomorrow."

"Where am I supposed to go?"

"I don't care. You're suffocating me. Go stay with Clara."

"But she lives so far away."

She waited in silence for me to leave. I stayed outside the door, sitting on the doormat.

I could have left for real, once and for all. I could have gone and spent a few days at Gaia's and then found some other place to live. I could have stayed with Diego, the brother of one of Flavia's girlfriends, who was always so nice and who lived alone. I should have left. But I stayed there and waited. Like always. I was a castaway on a desert island. I was the desert island. Two hours went by and she still hadn't opened the door. What if she really didn't want me there anymore? Would I really have to leave and start a strange, sad new life somewhere else? I was swept by panic. Would I have to break away from her? Would I ever be able to?

I thought about the parasites in chapter nine of the encyclopedia. The ones that inject infected bacteria with both toxin and antidote.

If the bacterium succeeds in killing the parasite and therefore recovers, its recovery coincides with its death. This is because the antidote leaves its system but the toxin persists and kills it. The bacterium cannot live without the parasite's genetic module: by now, the parasite is part of the bacterium.

I waited on the doormat with my heart in my throat.

After two hours, my mother reopened the door.

I went on growing.

I left my new inner foams on the bodies of older boys, stretched out in the seats of new cars or on the wet grass in the Parco Falcone, at night, with chirping crickets in the background. The first time was when I was fifteen, with an acne-faced boy from another class. He fucked me in the abandoned farmhouse behind the school, surrounded by overgrown underbrush shaped like taloned fingers, by the broken-in, worm-eaten door, against the low wall, next to a pair of rusty shears. I bled vertical, pouring down into the damp soil. On my way home, I kept thinking about the rusty shears.

I grew, and the dampness behind the walls of our apartment grew with me. It grew like some hidden blood, leaving wider and wider veins of gray patches. It grew and it crumbled the wall. The plaster fell to the floor like dead skin, I found small dark pieces of it on the soles of my feet. I grew but I'd understood the secret mechanism of grief. I'd understood that grief is a Russian nesting doll: it never ends, it just hides inside new grief, and every new instance of grief contains all the previous ones. So my grief was invisible but it was there, inside every stupid daily disappointment.

I grew and grew, without restraint. I grew like a tumor.

I understood that I should have died many years earlier, on my third birthday, the one I couldn't remember, the one where my father was there and then suddenly he wasn't. I knew that the picture on my headstone shouldn't have been of a young woman standing 5' 6", scrawny and a stranger to her father, with a scar on her nose from a fall on Mount Etna for which he'd never consoled her, and in her eyes billions of experiences he'd never know anything about. All the organic life that had taken me from the 3' 4", perhaps 3' 5", that I stood when he left me to the 5' 6" I had now attained was life infected, defective, an unnatural prolongment.

The picture on the headstone ought to be of the chubby little girl that he had left behind. I should have stayed that way, my face relaxed and wrinkle-free, like the untouched sheet in a dead person's bedroom. I should have stayed like a borrowed book: smooth pages, spine intact, just as it was, ready to be returned to its owner. I should have stayed like a fossil: buried in my dusty home until his return exhumed me.

When I turned eighteen, I saw Aunt Clara again after such a long time.

Her hair had gone back to chestnut and her second marriage was over. I came home from school, opened the door, and my drugstore bag full of antidepressants dropped to the floor: they'd hung up a green-and-red streamer that said HAPPY BIRTHDAY. I know where those streamers were sold, in the store downstairs from our apartment. Whenever I went in I'd look at them.

She and my mother had made lunch for me. That is, Aunt Clara had made it while my mother drank, most likely. They were sitting in chairs waiting for me in the dining room. Aunt Clara had cleaned the whole apartment; the floor was gleaming and so was the glass in the windows. As usual, they were a matching set: both had their hair tied back and both wore low-cut black dresses. When my mother handed me a slice of white-and-red cake, I smiled. Then I saw myself in the oval mirror behind them, the opaque mirror that was split in two.

There was no smile, no flash of teeth between parted lips. My mouth was closed, my face sealed like a zinc casket.

I went on growing. I continued to survive. The only reason a cell in our body grows and survives is because it is surrounded by molecules that suppress its instinct for self-destruction. On a cellular level, growth is a mischance. Our cells survive only through a chance bond, which delays and disguises their suicidal impulses. I met Lorenzo at a party on the beach and almost immediately fell in love. I was twenty. Lorenzo was thirty and had a watermelon-slice smile, large dark liquid eyes that feigned empathy, a muscular body, and straight teeth. He was pragmatic and taciturn, he had a fanatical love of insects and, in general, anything that expressed no emotions.

Lorenzo knew how to be just human enough.

His boilerplate affections at the movies left me with deep hickeys, his long fingers never wasted any time. An apartment-dwelling *Homo sapiens*, tame on the sofa but aggressive in the darkness of the flesh. At night, his sperm marked territory like a dog's pee. I'd open my eyes and he would no longer be on the bed. He was already in the shower; I'd hear water splashing, he would be singing songs I didn't know. Lorenzo was a friend to all and everyone was his friend.

The first time I saw him was on July 11, 2001, and I was at the Gloria Beach Club, attending my colleague Elisabetta's university graduation party. Everyone was in the water, splashing each other and laughing. Everyone had wet hair. There was a rock band from Misterbianco playing out-of-tune Radiohead covers. I was stretched out on the sand next to Gaia, who was telling me about a bartender she liked. I was watching Lorenzo, his dark eyes and his pointy, intelligent nose. I was watching

Lorenzo talk and smile and wave his hands in the distance, surrounded by people I knew but who had never become my friends. I got up and asked Elisabetta, who was wearing a leopard-print bikini and was vomiting up whiskey behind a hedge, to introduce us. The band was doing an off-key rendition of "Karma Police."

That night we fucked twice in his apartment on Piazza Galatea with the air conditioning set at seventy-two degrees. Then I fell asleep. I woke up with a start, in the middle of the night, to the sensation of tiny irritating spheres under my body. I had sand in the fold between my breasts, and all down my chest like a staircase of bread crumbs, and inside my panties like insects. Sand filled the bed, tracing a yellowish line from my sweaty back to his as he slept beside me. I turned to look at Lorenzo.

A streak of light from the streetlamps, filtering in through a crack in the ramshackle blinds, illuminated the wet grains along his neck and back and his folded arms, as tidy as a text message. I got out of bed. The parquet was covered with sand too.

When I got home I went to my mother's room, but the door was locked. I put my ear to the door: she was fucking someone. I went to sleep.

On April 23, 2009, two years and three months before my death, Lorenzo took me to the Isola delle Correnti, down the coast past Syracuse, the southernmost tip of Europe. A narrow strip of manmade rock, destroyed repeatedly by the waves, it marks the meeting point of the Ionian and Mediterranean seas. To our left were dark towering waves, to our right a sheet of water still and transparent as a crystal casket. And we were in the middle.

"I've done some research. There are a bunch of ghosts on this island because a bunch of ships full of illegal immigrants went down here."

"And you call that doing research?"

He laughed.

"No, but that's the most interesting thing about this place, don't you think?"

He laughed.

"Let's go, dummy."

A hole fifty feet deep gaped in the middle of the long man-made strip on which our bodies were standing motionless. We were there for Lorenzo's doctoral thesis: he was studying an insect that reproduces only on that island. We walked the length of that strip of rock, with the violent waves crashing one after another. Lorenzo went first, his shoulders as square and inviting as a chalkboard, his legs muscular. The water was icy, the wind was blowing hard; it was hard to keep your balance.

"Lorenzo?"

"Yeah? Need some help?"

"Lorenzo. Listen. You think I'm disgusting because I piss in my pants, don't you? I didn't want to tell you, I shouldn't have told you, I don't know why I did. Do you think that I'm a poor deranged girl? It only happens when I think about certain things. I mean, when I have certain nightmares. Do I disgust you?"

"You'll be better when you get some medicine."

"That's it?"

"Careful, the waves will pull you under."

He went on, and I trailed after him.

A very strong wind was blowing on the island. There were abandoned houses, with broken windows and grayish masses of dry vegetation surrounding them. At the center of the island stood the empty, weathered residence where, until ten years before, the lighthouse keeper had lived with his family. Lorenzo stopped in front of the place: a long white building in the process of falling apart. The saltwater had slobbered dark rust spots onto the building's metal sections. A sign warned us that we were in danger and forbade us to enter.

"Lorenzo, I have to tell you something. I love you."

He turned around.

Boxing up all your feelings in a single phrase is very convenient: it's an insurance policy against the mysteries of the subconscious. I relied upon that phrase where everyone takes shelter, that well-heated room where one can sit rapt in prayer. I relied upon my desire and upon my cloistered state within my desire. I trusted the self-abnegation that you could build inside, already thoroughly tested over the millennia by human animals on themselves: I thought I'd found safety.

"Aren't you going to say anything?"

"You know, this island is constantly being pounded by the waves, and they're always every bit as rough as they are right now. There are practically no plants, but look at this one, it's a wild leek. But the fauna is in better shape than the flora, there are wild rabbits and albatross. And then in the migration season, aquatic birds from North Africa pass through. If we came here then, just think, we could hide behind the dunes and watch them."

He entered the building. I followed him.

Inside it was dark, even though it was the middle of the day.

The light filtered in only through tiny chinks between the weakened rafters. The walls were flaking away; red stone appeared underneath here and there, like infected flesh. The floor was covered with broken white-and-blue tiles, dust, and dead spiders. We turned into the first room on the right. It had no door. With his back turned to me he squatted down to get a better look at a withered little plant that had sprouted between two muddy tiles. He remained motionless for a few seconds, the little plant plucked and held between his fingers. There was a syringe in the corner to our right, and on the wall YOU ARE MY LIFE was scrawled in red, half eaten away by briny encrustations.

The place reeked of damp. There was a dead mouse buried under a heap of white plaster. I left that room and went into the one on the left. This one had a door: it was ajar, and over it was another scrawled YOU ARE MY LIFE. In that room nearly all the rafters had given way, and a dense rotten-egg-colored light poured in along with the wind. Two chipped seashells next to the dust-laden doorjamb, which was covered with beads of mold. To the right was a spiral staircase. We didn't climb it.

On January 30, 2010, my second-to-last birthday alive, I woke up, took my morning pills, and went back to sleep. I powered down my cell phone to make sure no one could call to wish me happy birthday. I shut my eyes. At noon the door buzzer woke me up. Aunt Clara had come by with a cake and a present. She handed me the red package. I felt a chaotic warmth struggling to take shape inside me.

The gift was a secret diary bound in purple leather dotted with tiny white bunnies. It even had a lock. My mother arrived. She'd bought a beautiful yellow lemon cake with two little sugar figurines on top. It had birthday candles, one for each year, though it was two candles short.

I remember flying to Bologna to visit my mother's cousins for Christmas in 1990.

My mother wept silently with a book in her hand; the cover was orange and white. The clouds outside the airplane window looked like a motionless sea. A slab of dark waves, caught by surprise in the middle of a storm. Breakers suspended in that enchanted instant right before they crash down on the shore. You could see the entire arch of their bodies, the hook-shaped curve, soon thrust into the earth. A huge hand lifted to grab, as if full of yearning.

Yearning is what I miss most about being alive. But I can't say that I yearn for it: I lack the body to yearn with, the skin, and the mystery of warmth-bringing blood. All I have is a barren gaze, freed from my skull like a canary from its cage.

We were seated in one of the last rows in the plane and it was ten minutes to five in the afternoon. All around us people were moving: they gesticulated as they talked, they stood up to get something out of their suitcase or to use the restroom. Even the people sitting quietly reading were in movement: at a certain point, no matter what, they turned the page. Nothing could have persuaded them to sit motionless with their forefinger on the left page. I looked out at the sea of motionless clouds and the sun setting in the distance, a solid line that almost seemed to mark an end, a boundary. When they're alive, people are so free that they need boundaries. Both instinctually and culturally they identify boundaries with death. That's how it's always been, it's been that way for everyone, and it still is. People think that when you stop living, there's a bright line. Whether they envision it as a direct transfer to paradise or the simple cessation of all vital functions, they've always imagined this dividing line. They need that wall. They need to know that there's no knocking it down. No one has the courage to imagine it doesn't exist. Literature and religion have covered that wall with pious inscriptions.

The rip-off comes when you find out the truth. There's no wall, no dividing line, no boundary, no end.

The darker the clouds became the clearer the border became: a violent red against the false hesitation of black waves. Motionless waves equal desert. Desert equals thirst. Now that I am the desert, I no longer feel thirst, and I'm equal to everything else, as is the case with those who are no longer anything. I'm a free association, an empty figure, an untouched coloring book.

But even if I'm a gaze fluttering around freely outside of my skeleton, I can return inside my rib cage whenever I like. I can clutch the metacarpus and phalanges just as I did when holding hands was a comfort. I can do all these things because my skeleton and I love each other: we're in a kind of open relationship, and I'm jealous of all the insects, the wind and the rain, the anaerobic bacteria.

On February 23, 2010, two months before breaking up with me and fifteen months before my death, Lorenzo took me up Mount Etna. We were walking through the birch trees, taking the dirt road up to the Bocche di Fuoco, the "mouths of fire." Then we stopped in front of the Pozzo del Buio, the "well of darkness." It was a very deep pit in the earth. You could sense there were masses of dry leaves and other detritus at the bottom.

"I don't remember. Is this the cave where the ceramic vases were found? The one that was a place of worship in the Neolithic?"

"Shhh. If you stay quiet we'll see the tawny owl leave its lair."

We waited.

"You know, its best trait is its highly developed sense of hearing. It can hear even the quietest animals. And the tawny owl itself is extremely quiet. So the instant it hears its prey, it attacks, catching its victim unawares."

We waited.

Nothing emerged.

"That's hardly surprising. Daylight affects their nervous system, so in the morning they're lazy and slow."

Lorenzo descended into the cave. For a moment he vanished and I heard the sound of leaves crunching underfoot. He reemerged with a handful of black goop. His palm outstretched and his eyes glittering with excitement.

"Look at this, it's the skeleton and fur and teeth of a little mouse. The tawny owl is able to spit out all this and ingest just the organs, muscles, and flesh. Isn't that magnificent?"

Then we went to see his grandparents, who lived nearby, in Nicolosi Nord. They were very old. They lived in an orange

farmhouse, faded by the sun, half concealed by a mass of struggling vegetation. The living room window wasn't closing right,
and Lorenzo offered to fix it. Then he wound up the pendu-
lum clock in the dining room. He reset all the television chan-
nels. He oiled the lock on the back door. Sitting on the terrace
on a wicker chair, I waited.

2011

You see the dead. Or at least, you read them. You've become necroliterate. This is a letter that came to you by sea. And this is my death: there are still jellyfish, weeks, religions, city buses and post offices, concert tickets, clothes hangers, powdered chocolate, love letters, coffee umbrellas monkeys onionskin paper, sunglasses, elevators and weddings and hail, forks, store-window mannequins and real people, people and clothing, wool socks, dogs and hospitals, doors, door handles, boots and pillows, glass, leather, plastic, blood, cartilage, gums.

This is my death: the commercials on TV still last longer than the movies, people still go to work and at night they come home to their families. The streets are still congested but for me the streetlights are always green. Please, go right ahead, this is the apex of freedom, its narrow tip, as painful as a spearhead: you're invisible.

This is my death: my headstone is there too, a slab of rock surrounded by an assortment of flowers that I myself regularly see to replacing. I'm not actually sure it's my headstone: since I died I've forgotten how to read. I study my name up close and I can't say whether those marks say my identity.

But I still know how to write.

I know, it's odd that the two things don't go together. It's odd that this page I just wrote, now that I look at it, is a square of random shapes that I can interpret however I please, like those jagged inkblots in psychological tests. It's very sad: you write down your thoughts and before you know it they're no longer yours.

Focusing my eyes on my name carved into the marble, I can concentrate as hard as I like, but it's like looking out the window in the bedroom in Trecastagni, looking down at the olive tree in the courtyard, and trying to squeeze meaning out of every branch. I believe that branches, unlike letters, don't form words. I believe that the fact that the branches all derive from the same root does not imply that they have a semantic relationship. I believe that the leaves they cover themselves with in springtime mean nothing more than that: leaves.

I believe it, but I'm not positive.

This is my death: it set out from Catania, it's a universal geological phenomenon, but it's invisible. This is my death: on Mount Etna in winter there's snow, and on the sea below in the summer there are the dirty white wakes of motorboats. On Via Crispi there's a gray concrete apartment building that was built in the seventies, and on the fourth floor there's an apartment full of dust. Inside the apartment there's a mother crying over the kitchen sink, a bowl covered with meat sauce in her hands, soapsuds on her fingers. The water is running. There's an empty bedroom at the end of the hallway. There's a yellow bed, perfectly made, and biology textbooks piled high on the shelves. That mother is my mother: we live together, but I don't know how to reach her. That empty bedroom is where I live, but there's no proof of that fact.

My death began on the afternoon of July 23, 2011.

My name was deleted from the cell phone directories and Facebook contacts of a great many people. There was sorrow and tears, but outside of a certain geographic area only indifference. There was a funeral, two days later, and a body lowered deep into the earth. There was a thunderstorm, but only in the center of town: out at the Scogliera the sun was shining, and people went on jogging along the waterfront, music playing in their ears.

It's well known that the dead are obsessed with the regrets and resentments they accumulated during their lifetimes. And in fact the first thing I wanted to do as soon as I died was to go to Lorenzo's place. Even though a full year had passed since we broke up, he was my first thought as a dead person. The second was: I'm dead.

But what was I supposed to do with that death? Was it really such an important thing for me? That thing that art as a whole had been yammering on about, from time out of mind, I was now experiencing personally. I felt an enormous and uncomfortable responsibility. Having a body had given me the privilege of a restricted point of view, the opportunity to be irresponsible toward the vastness and mystical significance of the universe. But now, suddenly, I found myself a citizen of the Absolute, with all the seriousness attendant upon that role. Now the Tao and Nirvana were matters of day-to-day administration. Now the Zoroastrian bridge to the afterlife was every bit as relevant to me as the bridge over the Strait of Messina.

I woke up from life in the bathtub.

I got out of the bathtub: my dress was on the floor, and my body was in the tub. I looked at the clock on the wall: it was 7:21 P.M., and my mother still hadn't found me. I looked at myself: seen from outside, I looked nothing like myself.

I touched my puffy eyelids. My fine, thin dark hair, underwater from the earlobes down. My uptilted nose, with the scar on the right nostril from the time I took a spill off my mountain bike on Mount Etna when I was fifteen. A zit on my wet cheek. My small lips: the purple lipstick was still on. My wrist, abandoned forever over the rim of the tub, had left a round bloodstain on the marble.

I brought my ghostly forefinger near the stain. I established a contact. I reached the point where there was no longer any visible space between the pad of my fingertip and the stain. I pressed lightly. All this in life is called "touching," and it had a purpose and a result. I lifted my finger and looked at it: there was no blood on it. I repeated the whole operation: nothing. The stain lacked the generosity to give me a part of itself. The stain was not my friend.

I furiously plunged my hands into the sudsy red water. I pulled them back out: perfectly dry. Filth was a form of empathy that the world was no longer willing to offer me. Matter didn't understand me. I looked down at my bare feet: no, I couldn't feel the chill of the tiles at all. But why the hell should that surprise me? Without a body to act as interpreter, it was impossible to establish relationships with atoms and molecules.

"Now what am I supposed to do?" I asked myself.

No one answered.

I put the razor in the medicine chest, between the shampoo for brittle hair and the moisturizing cream. Outside the half-open window were the walls of apartment buildings, with laundry hung out to dry and lights turned on. It was 7:45 by now, and still my mother hadn't found me.

A moth fluttered in, zigzagged from side to side until it reached the fogged-up mirror, then flew back out. I picked up my black panties and bra from the floor, and my sleeveless red cotton dress. It was rumpled, shapeless. The blood had stained the neckline. I placed it on the sink and started scrubbing it hard with the tangerine-scented soap, the kind my mother always bought at the Body Shop. The stain was still there.

I tried using water, but it did no good. I kept scrubbing, making use of the terry-cloth towel. Down in the courtyard, only silence. The water kept running. I went on rubbing for half an hour, until the dress became wrinkled and hard. I continued until suddenly the fabric ripped. The stain was still there.

I kneeled at the foot of the bathtub that held my body, dipped the towel in the water, and delicately dabbed at my wrists.

It was harder to rub away the red clots on my right wrist: they were solid and substantial. They formed a pattern: when I was alive I would have instinctively identified them with some familiar shape. Living people don't do anything all day but find matches: they match clouds with animals, birthmarks with types of fruit, constellations with various figures, faces to other faces. Being just themselves causes such a great loneliness that people feel the need to seek not only their own kindred spirits but a kindred spirit for everything in the world. They look for doubles of everything. They even demand consolation for their own individuality from inanimate objects: not a cloud in the sky has the right to be just a cloud.

I left the bathroom and my apartment.

Out on the street I thought about how my mother was finishing counting to a hundred while Lidia was drowning herself in the river. I thought about my heart as it stopped beating. First one beat then another then silence. Having opened my wrists, I finally had eyes enough to see, but by then it was too late. Too late. Greta was walking barefoot on the rocks but Lidia was hidden forever. Too late. Greta was me and I was the river with Lidia drowning in it. I was my mother who didn't yet realize. There was no noise. My mother starts to understand. Then in the midst of the understanding come the pain and the grief, but it's still just an object, not the crowded piazza that it will eventually become. She doesn't know yet how it's going to work from now on. She doesn't know that grief will always be a stranger. She doesn't yet know the scalpel that will come every day to cut everything open, that nothing will ever be the same again, she doesn't yet know that she's already become an operating room.

On the banks of the Cassibile River, only cold rocks and dark trees in the distance, a beetle walking. Nothing yet been revealed; life still keeps its secret. Every color plays its own color, and every shape plays its shape. The colors and shapes haven't spoken yet. They haven't yet changed places, like in a game of musical chairs. There will be plenty of time for that; there will be lots of chairs, lots and lots of empty chairs.

It will start soon, and once it starts it will never stop. But now it's still the before. It's still clouds and flowing water and beetle on the rock, distant barking and translucent fish. An observer and the things being observed, like in a museum.

"Greta, Lidia! Where are you?"

The reality that was ending was a strange hide-and-seek, and everyone inside me had lost the game.

I wept the whole way to Piazza Galatea.

I was dead, and I felt the need to talk to someone about it. I'd selected the person who'd made me suffer most over the past few years: Lorenzo. I pressed the buzzer by his name over and over again. He didn't answer.

A crowd of young girls went past me, chattering loudly and dressed in loud colors.

"Hey, excuse me . . ."

It was a "testing, testing."

No one answered.

I should have felt devastated. Most important, I should have felt something. The 545 bus went by, and on the back there was a toothpaste ad, I remember it clearly: "Do you see blood when you brush your teeth? Try Sepsodent!"

Lorenzo wasn't answering on the intercom.

I went in anyway. I went upstairs to his apartment. He wasn't home.

But his new girlfriend was: her pictures and one of her scarves, in light-blue silk, hanging on the coatrack. A Tweety Bird mug with coffee residue inside it stood on the white wooden counter that separated the living room from the kitchen. A calendar of the two of them embracing in Taormina, set inside a pixelated heart. Every square announced an undertaking to be completed: never had a visit to Ikea struck me as so heartbreaking.

I picked up a pair of scissors: I wanted to throw the pictures at the wall and cut the scarf to pieces. I put the scissors down: I'm not that kind of a ghost. I'm more the kind who suffers and does nothing. The kind who keeps it all in. Like a shower drain.

In Lorenzo's office I found his new canvases (he's a painter in his spare time). They were all portraits, women's faces, all of them smiling, filled with a vulgar illusion. They were all the same woman, and the woman was the same as in the photographs. How could this be? Had he really fallen in love with someone else? I couldn't accept that. Being dead was depressing enough already.

The way he used to say: "I would never be able to make a serious commitment." It really is true that what does not kill you only makes you stronger. What does kill you, on the other hand, makes itself stronger, and suddenly Lorenzo seemed to have become a titan.

In the second drawer of his desk I found a letter written to him in a woman's hand, and that was when I realized death's worst collateral effect: I no longer knew how to read. Here I was, so worried about my unrequited love, suddenly caught in a tragedy of unrequited language. How could I survive without being able to read? Ah, right: I'd quit surviving. I thought about the other words with the prefixes "sur" and "over" and "super" and I realized that they were all over me, all above me. Overestimate, surmount, supernatural . . .

I no longer overestimate, now that I've seen the worst. I no longer surmount, because I'm always absent. I no longer imagine the supernatural, because nothing could be more supernatural than me. Those prefixes mean going past a certain limit, and I haven't crossed any limit: I'm the living proof that death is not a limit. I don't survive: I subvive.

In the bedroom I pulled the dresser drawers open.

That woman's clothes were in there too. Low-cut tops, tight-fitting jeans, the playful T-shirts of an overgrown teenager, other T-shirts that were his but that she without a doubt wore to work out in. It was obvious that this was a serious relationship; it wasn't just sex.

It was obvious that they were going to get married and they'd go to Morocco for their Christmas vacation and he would take a picture of her with a monkey climbing on her shoulder and in the photo you'd be able to see all the self-esteem of a person in a fulfilling relationship who was taking part in a bourgeois holiday ritual to be hung up on the virtual wall of a married couple's memories. They'd have two children, a boy and a girl, good students and nicely dressed, raised with all the indulgence and resources required to make them into the kind of human beings who confess their crushes and sign up for every kind of sport. The girl would celebrate graduating from high school with a trip to London with her best friends and in the streets of the city they'd laugh with the gratuitous laughter of tourists. As soon as the boy got his first girlfriend, Lorenzo would sit down with him to explain the importance of prophylactics without any idea that he'd learned this ridiculous ritual from American TV series.

I slumped down onto the gray leather armchair by the window.

"It's only reality," I told myself, *"it can't hurt you."*

Kids were coming home from nightclubs on their mopeds. Kids were strolling on the sidewalks chatting and laughing. The streetlights were all glowing brightly and so were the stars. I kept looking at the words of the letter the way you do with one of those colorful postcards that suddenly reveal a three-dimensional picture to you.

I walked from one end of the city to the other, for hours and hours.

I got home at three in the morning. My body was still in the tub full of blood. I opened the eyes of the me in the tub. The eyeballs had become more sunken and more glazed over. My lips were dry and chapped. I stretched out at the foot of the tub and went to sleep. When I woke up it was morning and I wasn't there anymore: the tub was empty.

I went into the kitchen and found my mother and my aunt.

My mother was leaning against the stove, sobbing in a yellow knotted sarong. The light was off. Aunt Clara was washing two white demitasse cups, silently. The two of them matched, both with mascara smeared down to their cheeks, and their hair stuck to their heads with sweat. Clearly they'd found me.

Now my mother had both hands pressed to her face. Her skinny arms traced a line parallel to her long, pallid body. How I missed parallel lines: the five-bar staffs of my sheet music, the pedestrian crossings to get safely across the street, the slices on my wrists before they were suffused with blood. I had never realized, when I was alive, how fond I was of geometry.

I went over to my mother. I wanted to give her a hug, but I no longer knew how. The void between her and me was suddenly an awkward obstacle. How could that be?

I looked at her, then I looked at my arms, undecided as to how I could best help them to overcome the distance between her and me. I held them out; perhaps I resembled a sleepwalker. Actually, I didn't resemble anything; you can't resemble when you can't be seen. I tried to move them, from my shoulders to my fingertips, but it was a movement with no destination, diffuse like darkness. Clara dried her hands and turned off the water. My mother dried her eyes but went on sobbing.

I gave up: I couldn't hug her. I stood with my arms in midair; I wept with her while she wept without me.

You can call me Dorotea.

But don't think that I'm one of those ghosts that come running when you utter their name. My name has already done its job. For twenty-five years it gathered me up completely: an unbreakable box, in which all the different parts of me were nestled in an orderly fashion, and they all snapped to attention every time I was pronounced, like an alarm being sounded. For twenty-five years, this box held me together, a single logo like on a package of cookies, a metronome for the cacophony of my identity.

No, you can't call me, I'll never come running. I was already a doormat in my relations antemortem, I certainly don't intend to go on being one now. Not that it matters all that much to me: I've moved past that phase of existence—life—where you care about things like pride and dignity.

At seven in the evening, in the dining room, my aunt poured my mother a glass of Chinese plum wine, and my mother said:

"Dorotea would have liked this."

In the soft tail of silence that followed, my name was against them. My name, two hours later, was the squeak of the bed as my mother tossed and turned, unable to sleep. My name was the silence in the hall when she got up to drink whiskey, and Clara appeared in the doorway in a pink nightgown and said to her: "That's enough now, Greta, that's enough." My name soon vanished from everyone's mouths, and when it did emerge, its breath smelled of alcohol and sleeplessness. My name is no longer in Lorenzo's thoughts, but it vanished from there long ago; now, however, it has also vanished from his cell phone directory. When my name is uttered, I don't respond: silence is my switchboard, it answers for me.

My name is an abandoned house.

The day after my death I got up at the usual time and went to work.

Via Vincenzo Giuffrida 63, stationery and gift shop. I crossed the street.

My boss, Mario Masi, a creaky seventy-year-old man with sunken eyes the color of dry ice, was sitting behind the cash register and looking at the computer. Suddenly there was something obscene and provocative about his elderliness. I walked in in a state of terror, of trepidation: would he be able to see me?

He turned around.

He smiled: he saw me. What a disappointment.

Sure, of course, that was what I'd been hoping for, but at the same time I found it disconcerting—now that my body lay rotting somewhere far away—to be mistaken for myself. It was a cruel affront for someone to attribute to me the very identity that I had annihilated with such an enormous act of willpower. It was an appalling show of disrespect.

It was also mere vulgar superstition: everyone knew I no longer existed. It was pure folklore. *I* was pure folklore. I was a relic of a popular lament. I was the cardboard protagonist of all the horror stories ever told in a dark campsite, in the glow of trembling flashlights. The vague shadow by the armoire that frightens the children at night. I was a misunderstanding, a horrible misunderstanding: where do you see the flesh and bones that were once called Dorotea Giglio, you idiot? Cut it out right now, you old lunatic, stop believing in me. I order you to stop. I don't exist, I swear to you.

"What are you doing just standing there? Get moving, you have the Moleskine notebooks to put away."

"Yes, I'm coming, Mr. Masi."

What alternative did I have? At least this way I could keep my job. All I had to do was be myself. A painless and legal act of identity theft.

I shut the door behind me.

The stationery shop seemed the same as before.

Small, clean, tidy, the multicolored flora of Stabilo pens on the right, the white ashtray by the cash register, the WWF calendar: July was still a panda. The ceramic umbrella stand from Caltagirone by the front door, with red-eyed white-and-yellow painted fish. The six spherical spotlights on the ceiling, the photo on the wall of the proprietor with his granddaughter in the garden: he's crouching down, sweaty and smiling, and she has a ring of chocolate around her mouth.

I put the Moleskines on the central shelf on the right, between the Paperblanks day planners and the Comix notebooks. My boss showed me a new line of notebooks made of recycled paper and then asked me to organize the Stabilo indelible-ink pens that had just come in, along with a box of Winx paintboxes. The electric lights were on: my boss's eyesight was getting worse. In fact, I'd been the only one putting prices on the merchandise for some time now.

But that morning there was something different about the electric light. It was a liquid thing perfectly contained by the shop's body, and the walls would never suddenly break open.

I did my work with my customary precision.

The newly dead, after all the thanatocentric advertising offered by religion and art, have enormous expectations concerning death, and I was no exception to the rule. That first day I anxiously awaited something extraordinary.

Two little elementary-school kids came in to buy a pencil sharpener and a graph-paper notebook. Then a stout lady asked for directions to the pharmacy. The phone rang: it was my boss's wife. Then at eleven he went to the café and came back with two coffees. Mine was a caffè macchiato, as always. I went into the bathroom and poured it down the sink. I returned to the counter with the empty cup.

"Ah, Dorotea, did you know that Amy Winehouse died yesterday? She was a great singer. You know her?"

I bit my tongue to keep from confessing that I too had died yesterday.

"Yes, I know her, it's true, she's great."

"*Was* great, you should say!"

Here's the worst thing about death: the inherent racism of human language. While the living gorge themselves on the present indicative, all we can hope for are moldy leftovers of the past tense. If you want even the tiniest helping of a verb in the present tense, you must necessarily have the obscene badge of a beating heart pinned to your chest.

"*Yes, of course, was. She was great. What a waste, to die so young.*"

I stood up to discard my empty paper cup.

"Hold on, though, don't you want to know how she died?"

"*Yes, of course. How did she die?*"

"They still don't know for sure, it might have been an overdose. Or maybe it was suicide."

"*I don't understand why someone would commit suicide, I mean someone who was so beloved.*"

That last thing was something I really thought.

"You know, Dorotea, what I can't understand is how anyone could commit suicide at all. Life is beautiful, and when you kill yourself you cause so much pain to the people who love you."

I looked at him. He was old. I wasn't interested in arguing about suicide.

After I got off work, I went to visit my violin teacher, hoping that he would see me the way my boss had, so that I could continue studying with him. I knew that he taught at the conservatory on Wednesdays, so I went to find him there.

I walked into his room without a word of greeting, because I was afraid I'd get no reply: I just picked up the violin and dove into a performance of Rossini's *O salutaris hostia* for soprano, violin, and organ. My teacher got a strange look on his face; he looked around in alarm. He went running out of the room, bumping into me as he went. It was clear that he hadn't seen me, but he had heard Rossini.

I left the room too.

I played my way down the corridor with its high, austere ceilings, past people who lifted their eyes to see where those sounds were coming from, as if in mystical ecstasy, and then continued down the hall. I'd walk into a room at random and start playing, hoping that someone would lock eyes with me and say something like: "Excuse me, but what do you think you're doing?" and then, hopefully, kick me out. I've never yearned so deeply to be kicked out, scolded, misunderstood. But it didn't happen, because no one saw me. Everyone took to their heels, some screaming, others simply with terrorized expressions on their faces, and sometimes they even turned the lights off on me. I wanted to finish my piece at least, and so I stayed in the last room.

I went on playing and I realized that I no longer had any need or desire to play. They'd already locked the heavy black front door with its brass handle. I passed through it.

It's sad to have no need of doors. It's sad to have no impediments whatsoever. Liberty is overrated.

When I got home, I found Dorotea Giglio in the living room, in a transparent casket.

Dorotea Giglio's eyes were closed, her eyelids were puffy, her arms were crossed over her chest as if in a straitjacket. I looked at her white face, her freckles. The nose was more pronounced, the skin had lost its color, my face was swollen. Her face. Our face. I was confused.

Relatives and friends, mixed together, noses dripping snot, leaned over the vitrine in which I was displayed. Some left filthy fingerprints. Aunt Clara was beautifully made up in pink tones. My mother was wandering around the room in a long dark-blue caftan and a pair of old sandals, not talking to anyone, drinking one glass of wine after another. Every so often she'd open the window and a blast of muggy heat steeped in yellow light would inundate everything, casting garish reflections on my casket. Then she'd shut it again. Every so often she'd ask someone if they wanted water, but then she'd fail to bring them a glass. Every so often she'd nod to herself. Every so often she'd even smile, but really it was more of a grimace. Every so often she'd go over to Gaia and Flavia or her cousin Emilia and stare hard at them. Every so often she'd wander close to me, but without knowing it.

I holed up in the kitchen and got some cheap supermarket table wine out of the fridge. I drank it: sliding over me, through me, it landed on the white floor tiles. I watched the dark-red puddle as it expanded, pushing beyond one tile and then the next, and then the next after that. It moved slowly, becoming grainy at the corners. I watched and waited for a cockroach to reach it, but it didn't happen. When everyone had left, my mother went around collecting the paper cups and Clara shut the curtains and the front door.

I lay down next to Dorotea, on the floor.

Behind the glass, I was beautiful. I'd never loved myself so much. I wished I could be me one last time, before it was the insects' turn.

I looked at the face, the freckles, the already dry lips curled in a sort of half smile: What the fuck do you have to smile about, you bitch? You think it's funny to have gone along with me, stopping my heart and my brain, just to support the naïve cause of my pain and sorrow? What right did you have to kill me, just because I felt lonely and useless and abandoned?

I looked at my face.

Her face.

No one's face.

All night long, hands clasped, I prayed to the oxygen to go on feeding my muscles for at least a little longer, to produce cellular energy and ward off rigor mortis. But the oxygen ignored me. At the funeral the next day, my body was stiff and cold, purplish. I had to leave the church without delay; I couldn't stand to see myself in such terrible shape. Later I held my body's hand as they lowered it deep into the ground. Relatives and friends left flowers on the headstone. I picked a little bunch of daisies from a bush and did the same. But I was the only one who had good intentions. The others didn't want me near them, they'd never again invite me to their dinner tables, they'd never again ask me how I'm doing and whether I'm still hungry, whether I'd like to spend the night.

It was dark. They locked the gates.

I availed myself of a ride with Aunt Clara. My mother was sitting in front, silent, her fingers busy scratching away an old stain from her black viscose dress. I got out on Corso Italia.

It was eight in the evening the way it is for the living: an hour followed by nine, not by a circus of eternity. It was possible to make plans for a Thursday at five thirty. It was possible to make an appointment for a manicure or make a stupid wisecrack or buy a pack of cigarettes. Two young men, one blond and one not, were transporting canvases: landscapes, women, hands. Two lovers held hands so they'd never lose each other. The windowed doors on the balconies were all open, the faces all looked out. At the Bar Europa a girl dressed in gray laughed into her phone, and a Moroccan held out roses to a couple who would not buy them. A glass was set down on a table, another was picked up and taken away. A young man with almond-shaped eyes looked at his appointment book while sipping a cappuccino. A cell phone rang, another was put away in a leather bag. The young man closes his appointment book. He's beautiful, with those high cheekbones and a supple neck.

He looks at me.

Who are you looking at through me, asshole?

My first visit to see myself was on Wednesday, July 27.

Wednesday was my day off from the stationery shop. I went into the cemetery, intimidated, looking around as if to ask permission. I walked down a broad street lined with large modern structures made of old cement.

I realized that I'd never been here before: the first time, I'd come in by another entrance. I didn't know which way to go. Behind the glass panes of the structures' facades there were dark rooms with drawers full of dead people. I came to a seven-story building. On the wall a modern sculpture depicted crowds of bronze faces with sad expressions, mingling together as they rose toward the ceiling, like fishing floats, the carved bodies lightened, like empty suits of clothing. I didn't remember them. I stepped into the elevator. I pushed the button for the top floor. In the elevator there was a cart loaded with dried flowers and cleaning products: ammonia, grease cutter.

From the seventh floor I looked down on the entire place and then went back downstairs. I retraced my steps and found the right entrance, the main entrance. There everything was different. Pine trees, palm trees, boulevards, traditional headstones. A bus came through and out of habit I stepped out of the way. It stopped amid the headstones. Two women got out, one young and one old, both brandishing opulent bouquets of chrysanthemums as if they were rifles.

I walked past small family chapels decorated to look like houses; behind the glass windows there were old framed photographs of big-bellied people in black and white, sitting at the table with cigarettes in their mouths. Then gravestones covered completely with earth. Graves without names. Graves topped by mutilated statues. One was a beakless eagle and a girl sitting looking at it. One was an open grave.

At last I came to my headstone.

I descended into the darkness of the soil. I climbed inside the wood, into the closed coffin, stopping just half an inch short of my body's outer wall. Here I am, here we are.

I opened my secret diary, the purple one with bunnies that Aunt Clara had given to me when I was alive.

I started writing on the first page.

07/27/2011: My face is swollen, my eyes are bulging. The skin is just starting to flake off my face. The cuts on my wrists have vanished. Horrifying lines have appeared where my arms attach to my body. Wide red tubes like deflated balloons. At first I didn't recognize them, then I understood. They're my veins. Germs have caused them to swell. They're full of disintegrating erythrocytes, red blood cells coming apart one by one, until finally they leave my veins as empty as the gutters of a house scheduled for demolition. I'm afraid.

From that day forward I documented my decomposition in my diary. Like a paleontologist, I documented what remained of my body from when I abandoned it. Its loneliness in the bowels of the earth and the worm invasions certainly didn't do it any good, but I didn't let appearances deceive me: I liked seeing my body open up, revealed little by little behind the flesh, like a confession. It was full of organs: that is the true meaning of inner beauty.

I went back up to the surface.

It was almost dark.

I went past dozens and dozens and dozens of graves. I walked down the boulevard, under tall gray motionless pines. Pines think themselves superior. Their branches look down on my brain stem.

When I got home I knocked on my mother's bedroom door. Silence. I went in anyway. It was dark except for the lamp on the nightstand. She was stretched out on her back, wearing red cotton pajamas. Her feet were covered with dust, her eyes were swollen, and she was staring into the void. I sat down on the edge of the bed, next to her.

"Mama?"

Silence.

I placed my hand on her left hip, where the cotton crept back, leaving a little bare skin. My mother didn't move: her skin couldn't feel my hand. I tried again: nothing. My touch was no longer requited.

"Mama, I'm afraid."

Silence.

"Mama, listen to me, I'm dead and I don't know what to do."

Silence.

"Mama, did you know that I can walk through walls?"

Silence.

"Mama, help me, my face is swollen and my arms are red and my skin is peeling off."

More silence. A curtain of silence pulled open shamelessly on a stage of silence.

Now a strange distance united us: a one-way mirror that on her side was absence and on mine intimacy. She remained motionless. For a long time. At a certain point she shut her eyes. I put my ear to her chest the way you might put your eye to the peephole in a door: *"Did you come to me? Are you dead?"*

Her heart replied: no, she's alive, beat it.

I went back to my bedroom. Outside it was raining. Lying on the faded yellow blanket showing Donald Duck and Goofy having a picnic in the countryside, I burst into tears. How odd: crying was so different now. Before there had been self-pity. There was also an emergency exit. Now instead crying was a bunker without so much as a window. I sobbed curled up in a fetal position, both hands covering my eyes. I cried loudly and then softly and then silently. Mostly I cried because no one was ever going to hear me cry again. I cried with my eyes squeezed shut, my arms wrapped tight around my knees. I kept saying: *"I want my mommy,"* like an abandoned child, but I was the one who had abandoned my mother. I kept saying: *"I want to go home,"* but I already was home.

On July 28 I left a message in lipstick in my mother's bathroom: "I'm still here."

I gave no credence to the rhetoric of an unbridgeable gap between the living and the dead. I didn't entirely believe in invisibility either. It struck me as a cinematic gimmick, perfect for Demi Moore moping around her apartment in overalls while her dead husband watches over her, unseen. What I needed was a solution, a translation, a way to go on being there. When my mother saw my message, she screamed.

07/29/2011: The network of swollen red veins that at first was limited to where my arms met my body has now reached my torso.

On July 30, just seven days after my death, the scene of my crime became a bathroom again. The blood was scraped off the white floor tiles and the tub was drained. A dark tangle of my hair was rooted out of the drain and tossed into the trash. The window was opened. Sunlight and fresh air and wind were allowed to enter. It was Aunt Clara who took care of these things.

On her knees on the floor, a scrub sponge in her hand, she tracked down and eliminated all traces of dried blood in the grooves between one tile and the next. In the meantime, my mother received her girlfriends in the living room, nicely made up in gray tones and wearing a blue silk dress. She showed them all a picture of me on the day of my First Communion: standing in the church courtyard, gloved hands clasped in prayer, a white lace dress a size too large, a palm tree behind me. Her friends passed the photo around in silence. My mother said: "That's Dorotea in her youth."

That bathroom was never used again.

I met Anna in the fruit aisle of the supermarket in Largo Pascoli, where I was walking and watching with envy and astonishment as hands reached out for peaches and apricots, feeling them, deciding which were ripe, and placing them in their carts.

She was sitting in a shopping cart. She had wrinkled cheeks, broad teeth, and salt-and-pepper hair. She was dressed in gray and she was slowly caressing a white-and-orange box of Kinder chocolate-covered granola bars.

Anna had died of a heart attack at age sixty-six. She ran a dry-cleaning establishment and she hadn't given up her business after her death. She'd put up a sheet of paper behind the counter that said AWAKE AND SING, YE THAT DWELL IN DUST: FOR THY DEW IS AS THE DEW OF HERBS, AND THE EARTH SHALL CAST OUT THE DEAD. ISAIAH 26:19.

"What's that?"

"Resurrection of the bodies. The Bible is very clear on this point. We shall rise again, Dorotea, we shall rise again."

I went home. My mother was on the couch, talking on the phone and laughing.

07/31/2011: The red network has spread even further downward. Red patches on my arms, my torso, my chest, my knees. Floats from the carnival in Rio, floats made of swollen and decaying superficial veins, spreading further and further downward, tinting my whole body red. It's not true that red is a lucky color.
08/01/2011: The network has continued to descend. Now it's denser than before and has turned black. I'm in prison.
08/01/2011: My brain has turned soft and yellowish. So long, memory, emotions, obsessions.

I went home and sat in a chair at the dining room table waiting for my mother. Two hours went by. A butterfly landed on my wrist, went through my wrist, all the way down to the wooden armrest.

I stayed there until she came home, got undressed, and went to sleep. I got up to make sure the door was shut correctly. I closed the window too. I turned the light off in the hall. I lay down next to her.

Every day when I came home from work I'd wait for my mother in the chair in the dining room, always the same chair, the one with the faint scratches on the wood in the right corner. When I was alive it always gave me a sensation of stickiness because of a peach juice spill that was never scrubbed off; now it no longer gave me anything.

Until the moment that she appeared in the dining room to get the wine, I remained there, motionless. "*Remain*" is the key word, if words could still open doors. "*Remain*" is the only word capable of describing me: the others are still on the side of the living. I write "*remain*" in italics. Italics have the angle of something stirred by the cold. Italics are an alarm. They say: *Be careful, you're in a zone of alienation, this is a word that's not like other words.* Italics see the dead.

While I was waiting on the first of August I wrote a letter to Gaia. The next day, before work, I left the letter on the reception desk at the real estate agency where she worked, but it was quickly buried under a pile of fliers and Post-its with the phone numbers of clients.

None of my postmortem letters ever reached their intended recipients, at least not in the common understanding of the phrase, which implies that someone realizes that the letter has arrived. That's because I myself am a letter that never reached its destination: the message of my body—with all its experiences and the things that it learned—remained buried underground, abandoned. It was lowered just a notch, from aboveground to underground. It was fired. Now it's unemployed, though it's certainly being employed by the bacteria. What a strange turnabout: before, my body had to eat in order to keep moving forward, now it's being eaten by insects in order to go backward, to retreat into nothingness.

Today is March 1, 2015, and I'm watching this slow last supper like a movie. A last supper without betrayal: everything is going just as it ought to; the universe is reappropriating its lost atoms. There are no unexpected turns or plot twists in the departure of these bones. The flesh is dismantled, the tissues come unstitched, and no bacterium ever withdraws from my body out of respect. Respect for whom, after all?

By now my inner life consists only of organs, and those are disintegrating. To say nothing of my skeleton. My skeleton is the building that survived the atomic bombing of Hiroshima: before it was a magnificent concert hall, now it's a monster of broken foundations. My eyes too are on the brink of extinction, surrounded by larvae: if I asked you what color they are now, you'd get it wrong. And what can we say about my tongue, which itself can no longer say anything? By now it's a dead tongue, just like Latin. My words are as halting as in a high school oral exam . . . *Rosa, rosae, rosae*? No thanks, not now that the roses crush me underfoot. You want me to recite the first declension? Not now that I too am in decline.

Aboveground, I watch my decomposition as if it were a film I don't like, in the background. I am the background, and I watch myself like a film. The film is one of those hyperrealist ones, without a plot, without beauty, full of silence and long takes along dirt roads. The film will come to an end, at a certain point: nature always meets its deadlines.

Soon Dorotea Giglio will be over, but don't touch that dial, stay on this channel: it won't be long before her atoms are recycled into a new human being!

You have no idea how cynical the universe can be.

In the meantime, as I watch myself decompose, I go on living more or less the same life as before. No, this is not a case of split personality: to have a split personality you must have a self. But I'm no longer myself: when you reach your posthumous years you lose certain limitations. I myself, or the world, go on as before. And to think that I expected so much from death. At the very least, a conclusion. I believed in an end. Deep down I was an idealist, and I had no idea.

You must be wondering: if I'm no longer myself, who am I? Well, I can tell you who I'm *not* anymore: my body. You can call me a soul, or a spirit, or a phantom. I don't know which term would be most accurate: science doesn't deal with these matters. Now it's all a religious question. You who are still alive can choose to believe or not to believe in me, just as I can choose to believe or not to believe in you.

I have a calendar.

It's ugly, orange and white, from the pharmacy on the corner downstairs from my apartment. January is the month of the tango, there's a drawing of a couple dressed in red, dancing against a vague light-blue background.

At night, lying next to my body, I flip through the months. I rip them from the spiral binding the way we once popped open cans of beer at parties, as if I were still invited to take part in the passage of time.

I mark crosses on the days, as if to take them down with me into the grave. I really need some company. But ever since I died, time has stretched out limply like a sweater in the washer. Time has become eternity, which is many sizes too big for me, and it just doesn't fit anymore.

On today's date, March 1, 2015, I write that the writer Violet Trefusis died this day in 1972. She died of malnutrition in a large villa outside Florence, overlooking a garden designed by her mother, surrounded by stone statues and poisonous dark-green boxwood hedges.

She wrote: "Be wicked, be brave, be drunk, be reckless, be dissolute, be despotic, be an anarchist, be a religious fanatic, be a suffragette, be anything you like, but for pity's sake be it to the top of your bent."

She wrote: "Live fully, live passionately, live disastrously."

I wait for her at the cemetery with a lemon cake, to celebrate the anniversary of her demise. We could talk about death, as would be appropriate in these circumstances. We could talk about putrefaction: it's the opposite of the old conversations about clothing, now that the body is becoming more denuded with every passing day.

The first few days back at work were really hard.

I had to come up with a bunch of excuses, saying that sudden bouts of panic kept me from talking to the customers, since the customers actually couldn't see me. Luckily Mr. Masi was a good-hearted old man who liked me, so he didn't fire me but instead agreed to limit my role to tending to the shelves. It was also good luck that he led a very solitary life and that he had a reputation for having an evil eye, and so he hadn't talked to anyone and he still hadn't heard about my death.

Whenever anyone came into the shop, I immediately hurried into the back, inventing some urgent task to attend to. The living hide when they don't want to be seen; I hide because no one can see me.

On August 2 at 5:00 P.M. a young brunette woman walked in and I instantly ducked under the counter. My boss saw me and when she left, he said: "What's wrong with you lately? You're out of your head!"

It was true.

It was such a relief, to finally be out of my head: when I was alive, I'd spent far too much time in my head, secluded in the chilly studio apartment of my brain, with all the broken windows and the locks that needed oiling. I suffocated in the stale air of my childhood, an unwilling roommate of all my past selves: I didn't have the keys to the front door. All the selves that were still alive and those that were on their way out and those that were already dead, trading clothes and skin with them, hanging their worms from my earlobes. Introspection is necrophilia.

When I got home from work, I found my mother and my aunt in their places. Sitting motionless on two identical chairs, with an empty one between them.

08/02/2011: The flesh fly has laid one hundred and seven eggs.
08/03/2011: The brain has become a gray-green mass. So long, reflection, ideas, logic.

Sitting next to my body, deep in the earth, I opened the calendar.

My favorite part was the "notes" section on the bottom right corner of each month. Where when I was still alive notations would pile up concerning shoes I wanted and movies to watch, must-see concerts and interesting exhibitions, because back then time was in short supply, and so it was exciting to shoehorn into that time various worthwhile commitments. Where notes flowed into each other about friends I absolutely needed to see again or even teeth that needed care, because back then things could go back to being healthy and nice. As I was leafing through it, a gust of wind tossed the pages: I immediately shut the calendar; I'd been found out.

My mother stopped cooking and worked less and less.
Aunt Clara came over for lunch and dinner every day: she

cooked, mopped the floors, and then went back to work. She planted geraniums on the balcony and hung a small Victorian painting over the bed of girls serenely strolling. She would ask my mother about the few photography jobs she did and remind her to water the geraniums. My mother would respond with a false smile. I never stopped having lunch and dinner with them.

As soon as they were done setting the table, I'd add my plate and silverware. The Winnie the Pooh glass from when I was small. The napkin. Each of them assumed it was the other who obstinately insisted on performing this daily ritual, and neither ever said a word for fear of offending the other. How sweet. Too bad that the cause of this newfound harmony had to be my death. I even said a prayer, a very new habit for me: I did it to give a phantom meaning to the silence. Or perhaps Anna had influenced me to some slight degree. Hands clasped, eyes shut, words that whether in my mind or in my mouth produced the same muted effect.

"Our father, who art in heaven . . ."

On August 4, my mother looked up from her plate of grilled chicken.

"At the park this morning, I dropped a lens; luckily it wasn't damaged. But the client—it was for a wedding—looked at me like I was an unfortunate lunatic. It wasn't my fault, you know, and nothing really happened. I just . . ."

She put her head in her hands and a tear rolled down her cheek. Aunt Clara patted her hand and poured a little more Nero d'Avola into her glass.

On August 6 at 2:08 in the afternoon, my mother accidentally knocked the blender off the shelf while reaching for the cheese grater. The blender hit the floor and came apart, its pieces scattering in all directions under the table. My mother got on her knees to pick them up and stayed there, bent over, staring at the pieces of plastic with a bewildered look on her face.

"It's broken."

Aunt Clara bent over to help her. She retrieved the base of the blender from under a chair.

"No, stop, Clara, don't you see? I told you, it's broken."

"We'll fix it, calm down."

"No, it can't be fixed, stop it, just look."

She pointed to a fragment under another chair: it was the corner of the lid. Clara picked up the chipped cover and tried to fit it onto the jar.

"You see? What did I tell you? Without that piece, there's no seal, it won't close, it's impossible."

"That doesn't matter, Greta, come on, we'll buy another one."

"I don't want another one. I want this one."

My mother took the two pieces out of Clara's hands and started fiddling with them, trying to force them closed with her fingers.

"You see? You see? It's no good!"

"Cut it out, Greta."

"It's no good! It's broken, can't you see, it's broken!"

"I said cut it out, Greta, put it down."

My mother wouldn't stop. Aunt Clara grabbed the cover out of her hands. My mother broke down crying.

08/07/2011, 7:42 A.M.: The one hundred and seven eggs of the flesh fly have hatched; obscene larvae have emerged. I refer to them as "107 Infestations," but it doesn't make me laugh.
9:42 A.M.: The larvae have gathered all around my dry lips. Never again kisses or insults, never again words.
10:00 A.M.: Silence.

Every Saturday I went to lie on the beach with Anna. All around us an expanse of dead strangers, inert, feet in the water, draped with seaweed, sometimes with gaping fish on their bellies, on their faces.

There was one crazy old man who dreamed up horoscopes for the dead. He would look at me, flat on his back, and say:

"Horoscope for Leos (those who died between July 23 and August 22): This year your death will be filled with discoveries, especially if you passed on between July 23 and August 2. If you died in an accident, look out for work-related accidents. If you died of disease, the virus of love might explode in your heart. If you died of old age, old friends will get in touch. But if you committed suicide, your death will always be a turbulent one, à la Night of the Living Dead: too bad for you."

I didn't believe in horoscopes. By then I was so unsuperstitious that I no longer even believed in feelings. I'd invented a more literal form of love. During kisses, we exchange hearts with our tongues. It takes the composure of a mummy and the exacting perfectionism of an Egyptian embalmer. It takes saliva as dense as the natron that the Egyptians gathered from dried lakebeds and then scattered over bodies gutted of their viscera. Literal love begins with removing the hearts from the collapsed caverns of our chests, deep underground, and swallowing them. Then the tap of the tongue, the sharp click. I tried it with Anna and she said: *"Never do that again, it's a sin."*

08/11/2011, 11:21 A.M.: All's quiet.
1:29 P.M.: Liquids of assorted colors.
5:01 P.M.: Flies, flies, flies.

At night, Anna and I would go to my place.

We'd sit on the sofa while my mother watched TV with Aunt Clara, and we'd chat. We'd play with my mother's hair. We'd count the strands, we'd braid them all over ourselves. We'd caress Clara's long red nails.

"Do you ever see your father?"
"I don't have a father."

"What about your mother, does she ever see you?"
"My mother doesn't have a daughter."

08/12/2011: Down there my body feels no regrets: the regrets have stayed with me, and I have to fight them off on my own. My regrets shrill, they whine, they throw tantrums, they keep me from sleeping. They disobey me. They grow. My body has enzymes instead of regrets. They emerged from the lacerated lysosomes and set about destroying their own tissues. And so every one of my cells crumbled itself from within, alone, in silence.
I initiated my own destruction, me and no one else.
The sporophytic microorganisms, the flesh flies, the cock-roaches, all the wretched frequenters of my flesh, open to the public, arrived from the outside world only later, to carry on the process of disintegration that I first began.

Hi, I'm Dorotea Giglio (1986–2011). We did theater together in middle school. I was the one who was three years older than you, I had dark hair and freckles, you remember? I'm the one who, that time we went to Milan to see the show about Pirandello, on the bus, told you about when my cousin's duckling almost drowned after it got tangled up in a piece of twine and the other duckling saved it by peeping really loud. You said it was a crazy story. Do you remember that? I know we didn't talk much for the rest of the trip. And I know that we haven't been in touch in the fourteen years since. But I heard that you died of leukemia, and since I was in your neighborhood, having died myself just last year, I thought that maybe we could get together . . .

I got your number from a girl who died of an overdose and used to do aerobics with you. I stopped by the hospital room where you stopped living, but you weren't there. I thought you might be in the morgue, hanging ribbons and necklaces on your frozen body, but you weren't there either. Nor at the cemetery; that's where I spend a lot of my time these days. Would you call me at this number? I really hope to hear from you. Ciao, kisses.

There was a gray concrete seventies-style apartment building. There was an apartment on the fourth floor full of dust. There was a mother crying over the kitchen sink, a plate covered with oil in her hands, soapsuds on her fingers. There was the water running from the tap. There was an empty bedroom at the end of the hallway. There was a yellow bed, perfectly made, and biology textbooks piled high on a shelf and a window that revealed the outside world. That mother was my mother: we lived together, but I didn't know how to reach her. That empty bedroom was the room where I once lived, but there was no proof of that fact.

The sheets were never sweaty, the mattress never curved under my weight. There was never a crease on the pillow. My fingers left no smudges on the windows. On the evening of August 14, looking out that window, I saw Gaia stop just short of the crosswalk in the street below and look up in my direction. I saw her look up and see no one.

I looked for myself in the bathtub less and less as time went on. Now I looked for myself in the streets, in the cafés, in the bookstores. Then in the Villa Bellini, the park where I spent so much time when I was alive. I'd sit on the edge of the basin and wait and wait and wait. I'd search the water with my fingers. Instead of myself I found one of the murdered swans. I think it must have been the last one; it was weeping in the center of the basin.

08/15/2011: It's rush hour on me. I'm not jealous of the bacteria. I remember clearly that all my life my body rejected their advances. But now it's different. Now it's better for my body not to be alone. And after all, my body and bacteria have lots in common: to be exact, 6.4 percent of their genetic material.

On August 18 Aunt Clara brought a jar of Bronte pistachio pesto for lunch. I opened the door for her, she assumed it was a gust of wind. She put her hat on the chair, I hung it up for her, she thanked my mother. When they were eating and she complained about the heat and reached for the bottle of mineral water, I blew on her neck. Not out of any particular altruism but out of frustration: I wanted to be responsible for things too, the way I had been when I was alive. But now my actions no longer belonged to me.

Everything I did the others always attributed to something else. Everything I did was split instantly in two: to me the cause, to expiate in my state of invisibility, and to the world the effect, an orphaned act that emerged out of nothingness. It was so unfair. Aunt Clara, after I blew on her neck, closed both eyes, the way you do when you know how to reopen them, and said with a smile: "I just felt the loveliest breeze."

09/11/2011: My cellular structures have definitively collapsed. All of the lysosomes have been razed to the ground like tumbledown shacks. All the cells have killed themselves, one after another, releasing horrible acid proteases.
Where is my self, amid all these disintegrating nucleoli? Where is it, poor earthquake victim? Where is it? Suffocated by the swelling of the mitochondrial structure? I look for it among the germs, all of them identical. I weep for it; I can just imagine it, a wet naked thing surrounded by mayhem. I so wish I could rescue it. I wish I could protect it from nature and carry it with me again, like a joey in a kangaroo's pouch.
09/15/2011: Outside it's still summer. Inside I don't recognize myself anymore.

On the evening of September 16, as usual, I went with Anna to go moonbathing on the beach.

There was a little dead boy with a nose like a potato and a gray T-shirt with blue stripes. He told me he'd been run over by a truck.

He was going for an outing in the countryside with his parents, but that wasn't actually true: they were just planning to abandon Dragonball, a Dalmatian-lab mix, which had no idea of what was in store and rode along with its white head out the window, eyes half closed. The little boy had no idea either. He knew his parents beat the dog whenever it crapped on the rug and were constantly complaining about how dirty it was. Then they stopped the car and let the dog out. The boy started shouting and sobbing. Parked in the emergency lane with the blinkers on, they put on their parent faces and explained that there was no alternative; he jumped out of the car and went running after the dog, which in its turn had made a bolt for freedom. The parents both leapt out of the car. They called the boy. The boy called the dog. Neither answered. Dragonball veered into the roadway. A truck went by. The boy was killed. Not the dog: it crossed safe and sound. The parents took the dog home.

"I waited there on the ground for months and months, but Dragonball never came back to me. He just stayed with my parents at home. I have a bad dog, he abandoned me by the side of the highway."

"What should I call you, by the way?"

"No, you shouldn't call me at all, jeez, don't you understand? Because the truck already ran over me. Tell my mother too, okay? Tell her not to call me anymore when she's sleeping."

Now the parents give the dog double rations of treats, and they take it out for a walk every two hours. Every time it craps on the carpet they burst into tears, surrounded by the pictures of the boy that hang on the walls: boy in the mountains, boy blowing out birthday candles, boy with parents on either side of him and green grass below him and smile on his face.

09/17/2011: The anaerobic germs, born inside me, have grown by now.
09/18/2011: My body, especially my swollen, taut belly, is covered with blisters.
09/24/2011: Some of the blisters have burst, releasing methane and hydrogen sulfide.
09/28/2011: More blisters have burst. Out comes hydrogen. Then nitrogen.
10/12/2011: My stomach has split open.
10/13/2011: The anaerobic germs have come to the surface. They break down the tissues.
10/16/2011: I can see my muscles.

In just three months' time my bathroom filled up with long cockroaches with quivering antennae and enormous weltering labyrinths of dust. A patch of green lime scale with dark-brown undertones spread out on the bottom of the tub, and an unknown spider constructed a web on the hot-water handle, and no one evicted him.

The ants too emerged from their holes and immediately attacked whatever food my mother left out of the fridge. There were cockroaches everywhere, lots and lots and lots of them. They moved over the walls like black lace curtains.

I picked up a handful of ants from the dining room table and a couple of cockroaches from the pasta drawer. I set the ants down on my sleeping mother's wrists, and the two cockroaches on her throat.

"Those look great on you. Now we're twinsies."

She woke up screaming.

Hi, I'm Dorotea Giglio (1986–2011). Three years ago you entered a coma due to a case of the flu. I don't know if you're still there, in your coma, midway between the two places, but if you've made it here I'd like to take you out for a pizza sometime. I tried to find you at your place, but you weren't in your bedroom. Your bedroom wasn't there anymore either. Instead there was a storeroom full of objects nobody uses anymore. A tennis racket, a pair of hiking shoes, a child's typewriter, an old television set, a bunch of discount bestsellers, and a Portuguese dictionary. Anyway, I think you're really cute. I'll be waiting for you at my apartment, on my bed. Ciao.

I saw Euridice for the first time on October 19, at the morgue.

She never told me her real name, but I didn't see why I would need it.

The morgue is a delivery room: Anna and I have loads of fun looking after the gestating bodies, sweetly awaiting eternity. They're so afraid, and they have no idea what's happening. We see them come in like hard, cold white dolls. Like Pinocchios who have turned back into puppets because they suffered too much as humans.

You can always glimpse a state of apnea in their eyes. Under the neon lights there's a fragile soul pushing to emerge from every cold body. It's difficult for all of them to find their way out, and the actual process of leaving the body is difficult too. And that's why we're there, to help them out. The medical examiner interrupts us: "The location and nature of the lesions demonstrates that . . ."

Or else it's a mother or a father who interrupts with their sobbing.

Ladies and gentlemen, silence, please, this death has just begun!

We explain to the dead how to manage eternity. We tell them that they have to go on sleeping and eating, in spite of everything. Watching TV, going for walks, pursuing hobbies, going out with friends. Life is neither good nor bad, but without the prospect of death on the horizon it's hard to muster much interest in keeping it going. Life goes on, as people say, and death too goes on and on and on. We watch as people come away from the world. It's an obscene doubling, not unlike birth itself, but less messy, without blood.

Congratulations, it was a boy!

We clap our hands, we scatter sky-blue confetti.

"What shall we call him?" asks Anna.

"But I already have a name, I'm called Fabio!"

We comfort the gestating souls, whispering in their ears: *"It's all over, you'll be out any second now."*

Sometimes we bring them presents: fake orchids, history books. Now they're empty and they're put away in their drawers, frozen: food in the freezer, ready for the worms' dinner.

That morning the body lying on its back belonged to a girl who had cut her wrists just like I did, and so I stayed very close to her, but no one emerged.

Euridice was sitting on the ground in her orange fake-silk dress, a visibly aging piece of apparel, with pilling and fine runs in the fabric, a ripped hem and patches of dry dirt. Her legs were covered with freckles, with intermittent patches of regrown hair, her feet were dirty and bare, and she was laughing at me. It was impossible to guess her age. She had long unkempt red hair and a notebook bound in purple leather in her hand. The medical examiner was bald and thickset, and he said: "A series of parallel wounds can be observed on the wrists."

And I said: *"Silence!"*

I looked at Euridice: she was writing, her dark eyes open wide.

The medical examiner: "This was a case of suicide."

"Silence!"

The morgue is an orphanage: you no longer belong to anyone, even your body has abandoned you. You need to accept that you're alone and abandoned to yourself, abandoned by your self. That you're no longer anything and that you no longer understand fuck-all because life no longer needs to be understood by you. That you've been rejected, that you're a discard, a discharge of rational thought. Because all we are is brains under glass: the glass is our body, but even more transparent. You no longer understand: you invent. Without senses, reality is no longer on offer. Understanding is an auction: you raise the bid with an interpretation, hoping that it's accurate. Understanding is like tossing a pebble into the water. Mine always sink to the bottom.

The good thing is that now that rational thought is no longer a train traveling toward the truth, it's no longer frightening. So we no longer take refuge in the irrational. We no longer feel the need to believe in God and love. At Easter we play the game of nailing our hands and feet to the wall, laughing and laughing at how little it hurts. We tell each other our sins in order to appreciate just how pointless guilt is, and how much more pointless forgiveness is. On Valentine's Day some feed their hearts to the dogs, since by now they've gone bad anyway.

That night, at the morgue, I leaned over to read the tag that dangled from the foot of the newly dead girl, but of course I couldn't decipher it. I left the room.

Later I saw Euridice again in Piazza Teatro Massimo: she was drinking an orange vodka that collapsed through her onto the asphalt. She was talking with Anna.

"This is Euridice."

"Yes, I saw her this morning at the morgue."

And Euridice said: *"You look prettier tonight."*

I learned that in spite of her childish appearance she was more or less the same age as me. She asked me a few questions about how I'd killed myself, the number of razor blades and the water temperature in the tub, but she wouldn't tell me anything about her death. Then we moved on to the subject of shoes.

Euridice wasn't her real name, that was her pen name as a deceased novelist. I decided immediately that I liked her a lot, that she was a sensitive soul. We would have been best friends for life, if we weren't already dead.

Everyone called her *Euridice la scrittrice*, Euridice the Writer, because that's what she wanted to be called. The rhyme was intentional: now that our words no longer communicated anything to the living, we took great enjoyment in making our words communicate with each other. A rhyme was a perfect coming-together for them, their version of love at first sight, of incest on a desert island. It was the only available form of dialogue, specially packaged just for us. It was a cover that fit perfectly with its box, and that was especially important, now that the box was empty.

Euridice remembered the names of her classmates from high school and a list of her favorite books. This filled me with astonishment and admiration. Memory among the dead generates the same reverential respect that prophecy does among the living, because it's a way of processing time that is extraneous to us: certainly, we still remember the events of our past, but not the minor details.

Euridice was writing a science fiction novel. The main character was called Euridice, and she was a human being living on a hostile planet called Earth. *"Her mission is to go on living without killing herself, and she will succeed because she's a superhero."*

That told me that she too had committed suicide, but I decided not to ask any more questions, since she clearly didn't want to talk about it.

Since meeting Euridice I felt less lonely. As if I'd expected her. Certain mornings I felt the way I did before I putrefied. I felt my heart inside and the world outside, as if there were nothing missing, not even the future.

November 2 was the Day of the Dead, and the cemetery was absolutely packed. Leaning over the coffin, squeezed in among the crowd of conventionally prostrate relatives, I rooted for my corpse: *"Rise and walk."*

Genuflecting old women and bored kids, spouses carrying flowers wrapped in vulgar aluminum foil. How uninteresting, the ritual of visiting the dead. With my gaze focused on my body, I kept saying to it, over and over: *"Get moving!"* I was rooting for it as if at a horse race. It wanted to be Lazarus, the same way it wanted to be Sailor Moon when I was small. Its eyes were closed as it wished for its transformation, but now it could no longer open them.

I needed to resign myself. It wouldn't be coming home even for Christmas, nor for my birthday. I'd have to celebrate without the cheeks to blow out candles or the hips to dance. Without a stomach to digest the cake or the lips to say thank you. Other people's kisses wouldn't smack. I'll have to celebrate without my body: it's no longer invited. Without it, I won't be able to turn a year older: it was my body that always kept count. It was my body that proved that time went on and on and on, and it was also the reason that it did.

I'll be stuck with my age of twenty-five, as well as with the same old dirty dress. Like a panhandler in an American movie who jealously pockets the only quarter he's made all day, I'd eke out the rest of eternity with my quarter century of life.

I went home. My mother was sleeping naked with the light on and a romance novel open on her belly. I tucked her in.

On November 7, like every Monday, there were plenty of customers. High school students making tiny Xeroxes of their art history textbooks to hide during their in-class writing assignments, little kids from middle school who needed official paper for bureaucratic requests, but also professionals who needed Xeroxes, envelopes—in other words, objects that would only temporarily be in their possession, and so there was never any emotion in their voices when they asked me for them. Which is why I wasn't very interested in this type of customer. The ones I cared about were the elementary school children who asked for notebooks. When my boss would point them to a shelf, they'd spend a long time picking one out, with considerable trepidation, reviewing all the covers available, as if they were choosing something they'd use for the rest of their lives. That morning a dark-haired little girl was unsure whether to pick a graph-paper notebook covered with teddy bears and little hearts or a more masculine one with a picture of a guy surfing. I hid behind the shelf and watched with a smile.

When I got home my mother was already asleep. I gave her a goodnight kiss.

Now that there were finally insects at my place, I got into the habit of leaving a trail of sugar on the dining room table every evening. Then I'd come home late at night and turn on the light. I'd watch the cockroaches scatter across the table like inkblots, I'd watch them take refuge in the corners: they knew I was there and it didn't strike them as absurd. They believed in me, and in return I believed in them.

11/10/2011: Life is hard up here without my body. Down there time is running out and there's nothing I can do about it. If I'd known that my vanity would be transformed into a pathetic unrequited love, perhaps I'd never have killed myself.

On November 12, Anna met Filippo.

She won his heart in the pub on Piazza Teatro Massimo: she went up to him and said: *"Ciao, I believe in love and friendship, and above all in respect."* To believe in something is one of the sweetest things that can happen to a dead person, and it's an excellent weapon of seduction. And so that same night they went to a hotel on Viale Regina Margherita and had sex.

Anna isn't pretty, but she had a beautiful death that left no marks. She died in her sleep: heart attacks, like idealism, are also a tool of seduction here. My slashed veins aren't much to flaunt, on a Saturday night, while I drink my usual whiskey at the pub on Piazza Teatro Massimo. In fact, people here dislike suicides. We're the pariahs of the deceased community, and they avoid us like the plague. We are the ones who discarded the only thing they desire. Just try and make them understand, understand that when I was alive I loved life much more than they ever did, that they're a bunch of hypocrites for changing their preferences only afterward, like children after you take their ball away. Try and make them understand that while artists can recycle their suffering in their art, I didn't know what to do with mine. The things that you don't know how to use don't belong to you.

I want another whiskey. Euridice steals a bottle for me from behind the bar. I raise the bottle: I drink with her to all the goals we can no longer achieve. As soon as I raise my wrist and it comes close to the candle, the cuts are illuminated: it's my empty pentagram, I'm fond of it, all my silence is written in it.

That night I went to the hotel on Viale Regina Margherita with Anna and Filippo. It was a small room that overlooked the empty street. It was very quiet.

While they were getting undressed I went in the bathroom and unwrapped the little soap bars, arranged on a little dish next to the packets of shampoo and bodywash, and I held the bars in my hand for a while, caressing them. I could feel the impression of what had once been deep emotion. Its empty, gaping form, without anything left inside.

In the hotel room I sat on a chair and watched them fuck.

She lay on her back and he climbed on top of her.

They started slowly. Right hand on right breast. Fingers clutching. They mimed gestures that were miles and galaxies away. Gestures that they remembered mathematically but not emotionally. Not the electric discharge of nerves, not the marathon of blood. Then the parts fit together: that still worked. Back and forth, without sweat. Back and forth, without expecting anything more. They shut their eyes tight. Her fingers followed a familiar route over his back. Their mouths knew the equation of tongue and lips but there was no saliva available. They held on to each other desperately as if on a sinking ship, she clamped her skinny thighs around him but their solitude didn't change temperature. There was no sweat to secrete, no sperm to spill. I looked out at that desert, with concentration and a bit of pity. There were even moans at the end, like the ones they'd seen themselves emit when they were still alive.

They were reproducing a counterfeit desire. They dressed in silence.

Now instead of desire there's a desire for desire. Now inside the bodies there are no ovaries to be deceived, no lungs to make us pant. Now sex is the body's own empty room inside the empty room of a hotel. There, that's what death is: a matryoshka doll of empty rooms. Too bad, now that love really would be eternal.

Then Christmas came.

Aunt Clara put up the tree and strung it with Christmas lights. On Christmas Eve she made lasagna and my mother put on some easy-listening music. They didn't say a word during dinner. They each wondered who had bought the napkins and the red forks. They each wondered who had put a silvery star of Bethlehem on the tree. They each wondered who'd lit the incense and who'd cleaned the jam and crumbs off the table. They each wondered why the floor was gleaming and the windows were sparkling.

After dinner I went to visit myself at the cemetery.

I dragged my body out of the coffin. I decked it with red and green Christmas ornaments and little wooden angels. There was a red toy train dangling from one rib, a Santa Claus lodged in the eye, a Baby Jesus nestled cozily in the jawbone. Spook lights were our crackling hearth.

At a certain point the rats arrived, even though no one had invited them. I was tempted to chase them away, but it would have been an act of selfishness. Unjustifiable arrogance. Now that I was incorporeal, my body had much more in common with the rats than it did with me: to be exact, they shared 94.9 percent of their genetic material.

Euridice showed up.

"What are you doing here?"

"But you invited me yourself!"

"Yes, but I never thought you'd come, you said that you were going to write all night."

"I've already written everything I wanted to write. It's a true story. I can read it to you from memory."

"Okay."

"At Sungir, near Moscow, a young woman, a man, and a little girl were buried thirty thousand years ago. Their bones were shuffled together like a pack of cards. Like that game where everyone's an animal: who's the calf, who's the carotid artery? The foot pretends to be a hand, a rib claims to be a sternum. Skull against skull, the bones were arranged in lovely rings like oversized necklaces. Between a leg and a sternum, between an eye socket and an orphaned hand, precious jewelry and little sculptures of horses were placed, alongside little ivory outfits and straightened mammoth tusks. The girl's skull was adorned with lots of tiny beads. The mammoth tusks were like the sides of a toy chest. Inside the chest, the bones played at being playthings themselves. 'To be or not to be,' asks the skull, but everyone knows the answer. Unfortunately, thirty thousand years later, those happy bones were placed in a museum. And so they discovered that they weren't a toy chest at all, but a historic artifact.

They never would have wanted to be anything so serious. 'We are a relic of the human race dating back to the Paleolithic,' says the rib cage sadly, 'and there's nothing fun about that.' In that museum the bones were very depressed."

"Is that how the story ends?"

"What else were you expecting? Now let's have a smoke."

She pulled out of her pocket a cigarette for herself and another for me.

I lit mine and imagined that puzzle of bones. I lit a second cigarette and imagined the bones after they'd been arranged for display in the museum. I lit a third and imagined that I was at the museum and then I went out and did lots of things because I was still alive.

With every cigarette an image, just like the Little Match Girl on Christmas Eve. And like her, after the last cigarette, I died: nothing new there.

12/27/2011: My body has gotten smaller, or else the coffin has gotten bigger.

12/30/2011: The aerobic germs are new in town and they attack the tissues that my anaerobic germs have crumbled to bits.

O n New Year's I went to look for myself on the bed of the Cassibile River, where Lidia drowned herself. Anna and Euridice came with me.

We ventured all the way to the lakes. I plunged my arms into the water. My fingers into the mud. I excavated, I probed.

Euridice: *"Did you know that in the old days the cavity in the heart where blood gathers was called the lake?"*

Euridice: *"Did you know that our hearts pumped seventy-five milliliters of blood with every beat?"*

I searched underground as well. Now that my body no longer enclosed me, I could be everywhere and anywhere. I scratched the bark of the pine tree Euridice was leaning against and checked the liquid that oozed out. I crushed seven ants with my shoe to see their red. My blood could gush out anywhere: anatomy has become geography. My blood secretly irrigates the parched hills.

Anna: *"The new wine mourneth, the vine languisheth, all the merryhearted do sigh."*

"Quit quoting from the Bible."

"It's Isaiah and he knew very well that the world would end and then begin again. Now we need only wait for it to begin again."

My blood at the base of Mount Etna, subterranean, hemmed in by rock. My blood that pushes up from under the stalks of plants and the roots of oak trees. Clotted inside each plant, dried in the open mouth of every red petunia. To breathe in, now, is a gust of wind.

The myocardium makes the mud pulse all the way to the slimy bristles of the earthworms, to their tiny mouths that suck at the dirt and the seeds and the eggs and the fragments of decomposing plants. The aorta pushes the worms out of the soil, into the sunlight. My tissues, once they've decayed, will garb the entire island: a garment of flesh stretching all the way to where the sea begins. The intricate corals of my arteries, I remember, were sixty thousand miles long: if you link them all together and wrap them around twice, they'll adorn the throat of the Earth's entire surface. When I grow up I'm going to be the world. When I grow up, and my body has vanished, I will be petals and murky rivers and endless eyes and ladders made of spread fingers and smoke-ice-eyelashes-bark-hail-wool-liver-iron-moon-fly wings.

It's just a matter of time; my innards are already spreading like a true story. Through the mud as if by word of mouth, a rumor made up of rotted glands. By now the arteries can no longer keep the secret to themselves: everyone, take, drink, this rain and these lakes and these rivers are my blood.

Anna: *"They shall not drink wine with a song; strong drink shall be bitter to them that drink it."*

It started raining. I looked up but the water wasn't red. Euridice had stopped talking. Her face remained expressionless.

"Listen, exactly how long has it been since you passed away?"

She lowered her eyes to her notebook and started writing.

"Hey, are you listening to me? Or are you still underground?"

She went on writing.

"Please, tell me."

She shut her notebook and walked away. I followed her along the rocky walls.

"Leave me alone, Dorotea. Go away."

"No, I want to know. I also want to know why you never go to visit your body."

She turned around, her eyes staring, her gaze cold: *"If you don't leave me alone, I'll go to your house and throw all the photographs against the wall and then I'll slam all the doors and then I'll scare your mother to death, I'll make her scream until she pisses herself and her vocal cords explode and she loses her voice for good. I'll chase her to the window, I'll shout in her ears, I'll make her jump out."*

I fell silent. I watched her walk away.

Every now and then, while I was lying in bed at night, aping the things that living people do before they go to sleep (listening to music on an iPod, leafing through magazines, looking at the ceiling), I'd find myself engaging in what had once been thoughtful reflection, but was now rummaging around inside myself, groping around in the dark. That inner process that once led to an understanding of the world now rammed its head blindly against the imagination.

There was no way out: on those walls, the ideas were frozen like prehistoric engravings, hieroglyphics inside a tomb, drawings that never meet the things they depict. My mind was a furious whirligig of puzzle pieces that never stopped to form a picture. At times they'd slow down enough to create the illusion of an image: a face, an idea, something real. Then I'd say: finally, I understand. Blood is red, my mother is a brunette, my mother loves me.

But then I'd discover a monstrous lie in that harmony: the puzzle pieces were in the wrong places. Misunderstandings are the gaping edges of whatever it is we call freedom: without my senses, I was so completely free that I could interpret everything in whatever way I chose, without the constraints of perception. Reality was an extinct wild beast, and I could give it all the names I wanted. But names weren't good for much, without my senses to call reality to me.

Reality was useful only to the others. Supine on my bed, I wanted to get angry, but even the stones of my anger, rather than manifest themselves in shouts and fits of rage, remained inside me like kidney stones.

How I wish I could actually reflect.

But now to "reflect" was a treasure map to a lost privilege, so lost that it had become legend to me. It was a mythological verb: it was trapped inside a labyrinth without even being able to find the minotaur. It was set within quotation marks that weren't even the same as those of the dialogue. Now I reflected without understanding, meaning I wasn't reflecting at all anymore. It was a game of snakes and ladders: every time I misunderstood I'd lose my turn and be sidelined forever. Now I reflected the way mirrors do: whatever they find within themselves, they never understand its meaning.

On January 4 I went to the cemetery with Euridice. After watching my decomposition for half an hour, she said: *"I have to tell you something. I like your body. It's really lovely."*

"Thank you."

"I'd like to keep it. I'll take it to the movies with me, I'll confide my secrets to it, we'll have dinner together every night, and I'll dress it in yellow and red. I'll tell my friends it's my sister."

"What are you talking about? You can't do those things with my body!"

"It will be a character in my novel, Euridice la Scrittrice's best friend. It will help her on her mission of escaping suicide. My book will be a masterpiece."

"That's enough of that. You're talking nonsense, you can't do those things with my body, I told you."

"Why can't I? Who says?"

"It says so right here, on my headstone! It says that this body was called Dorotea Giglio, and I'm Dorotea Giglio, I was her, and now she's no one."

"I can't see anything on your headstone but marks that mean nothing."

I got up and left.

By the main entrance, next to a pair of weather-beaten head-stones, stood two dead girls. Black hair, immaterial bodies dressed in pastel-colored summer clothes, and next to them their little exhumed skeletons. They carried armfuls of pupae. They'd rock them slowly, then put them back to bed in the holes of their lips.

I left my headstone and went to Lorenzo's apartment.

He wasn't home. The apartment was empty.

I walked through dark rooms, touching things. In his room I opened the second dresser drawer, where he used to keep our loose photographs. They weren't there anymore. Just pencil sharpeners and fliers and paper clips and a leather desk diary that had never been used. Where were the two of us at Vendicari, with a flamingo beside us, and him in a pair of goggles with a seashell in one hand? And us hiking up Mount Etna, in heavy hiking boots, with tired smiles? Us in Barcelona in front of one of Gaudí's undulating facades?

I was so tired. I was so tired and I was tired of being tired in the past tense, I wanted to be tired in the present. Instead, even tiredness is in the past. I'm not anymore—I was and that's that.

Oh, how I miss the present indicative. To be able to say "I live here" or "I'm going to the movies." Actions under way, tall and muscular and clothed in possibility, whereas now actions are stiff, naked fetuses, just completed and already sealed in little caskets for children, without any right to engender consequences. Nostalgia for when hope had some logical meaning, projected as it was into the future. Now it walks backward like a crayfish, and however much you might hope, what you're left with is never any different from things as they happened.

What I miss most of all is missing things. Remembering the past isn't heartbreaking or romantic anymore. It gives no comfort; it's just a form of calisthenics, or even worse, a muscle spasm.

01/05/2012, 2:03 A.M.: My mouth is falling. My whole face is falling. I'm falling apart. My cheeks are puffy and full of keyholes. The rest of my body is swollen and corroded too. I'm falling apart, I'm falling apart. Lorenzo threw away his photos of me.

2:43 A.M.: No, I didn't die of love. I really wish I had: I'd be carrying on the legacy of literary figures like Anna Karenina or Emma Bovary. Instead, you recover from love. One day you wake up and the heaviness you felt in your chest is gone. Another day you find you've stopped thinking about it. You start living again, without rancor, like a lamed dog. And what could be sadder than that, that your love wasn't meaningful and powerful enough to persist? That a blind biology, responsible for your survival, should have uprooted your passion like some tremendous typhoon? The foundations of love and trust upon which you built your home have been destroyed. Just as the words spoken under the covers and the dreams of the future and the sacrifices with which you furnished every room have been destroyed. Something healthy and sadly primordial inside you, something that is yourself much more than you ever could be, has devastated every piece of furniture, every wall, leaving you frighteningly free and alive in the middle of the world. I faced up to that something. That typhoon, that biology. I faced up to it, and I beat it. I won, I won, I won a bunch of insects. I won the butterflies that tear out my hair, one strand at a time: he loves me, he loves me not.

And I go on winning: the Dermestes lardarius *arrived today of all days, delivered to my doorstep, right to the heart of my flesh. God, I've won so many insects you wouldn't believe it. I won flesh flies with big black eyes and striped wings.*

*Swarming on my lips like lipstick, they strip them of flesh
until they're gone. Silence: the flies are my last words. Silence:
the awards ceremony, deep underground, is still under way.*

On January 9, my first day back at work after the holidays,
my boss said to me: "Sit down."

"I'm fine standing up. What is it?"

"I just wanted to tell you there's no need for you to go on
pretending with me, I figured out months ago that you were
dead."

It came as a shock; I had nothing to say in response.

"You know, I wasn't that surprised when I found out. My
wife has never left me, not even after she died. Someday I
ought to introduce you."

"Am I fired?"

"Eh? No, no. Of course not. You know how fond I am of
you."

"Sir, you're the only person I know who can see me."

"That's enough now, you're making me blush. Now go
organize those packs of paper, it's already ten o'clock."

When I got home, my mother was on the couch with a
strapping big man with a beard.

His skin was pockmarked and his eyes were enormous.
They were drinking cheap wine and she was laughing at his
stupid jokes. He had a pronounced accent from another city
not far away, and he was eyeing her lustfully. I sat down next
to them.

I listened to them talk. My mother was wearing a long emer-
ald-green dress that had been washed too many times: the fabric was pilling around the boat-neck collar. I got up and went to
take a look around. There were empty plates on the kitchen
table and an empty baking dish coated with tomato sauce. There
were crumbs on the floor and dark patches of grease on the

stove. In my mother's bathroom, her IUD box sat empty. I went into her bedroom and lay down on the bed to wait.

Outside there was silence, except for the sound of traffic, which never changes: whether I was a little girl, a grown woman, or dead, it was a sound without a message. On the dark-walnut nightstand was a black-and-white picture of me when I was just a few months old, in a pair of denim overalls, with a pacifier in my mouth. Then there was a violet scarf and a Moroccan jewelry box full of rings, some of them valuable, others nothing more than costume jewelry. On the wall was the Victorian painting that Aunt Clara had given her: two girls in the countryside seen from behind, though their joy was unmistakable. Then there was a print that Aunt Clara had given her: *Dulle Griet*—"Mad Greta"—by Brueghel. A tall skinny witch runs straight toward the mouth of Hell, her hands full of stolen jewelry. All around her the city is in flames, ravaged and overrun by monsters.

The door swung open.

They came in: they were kissing and they were tipsy. She was laughing too hard and her hair was a mess. He shoved her against the wall and lifted her thigh; he kissed her on the mouth and on the neck, long and hard. She went on laughing, then started panting. He unzipped his jeans. She slipped away and took off her dress, her worn black-lace bra, her panties. She lay down on the bed next to me.

Some nights, on the seashore, Euridice and I would play an exciting role-playing game.

The game was called "life." We'd play the roles of two living people with their future ahead of them, just waiting to accommodate their plans. It was a little bit like the parlor game "I'm going on a trip and I'm going to pack," but the winner was the one who told the biggest whopper.

She said: *"Next year I'm going to compete for a literary award."*

I said: *"I'm going to go on an organized tour to Indonesia."*
She said: *"In two years I'm going to enroll at the university."*
I said: *"I'm going to get married."*
And then she, in a serious voice, with her cunning eyes looking straight at me, said: *"I'm going to have a baby."*
She had won.

Hi, I'm Dorotea Giglio (1986–2011). We went to elementary school together. I was the one with freckles. Do you remember that time at Luigi's party, Luigi from class 3C, when we invented a cocktail made of Coca-Cola and jam and peach juice? It was disgusting. I know that we haven't seen each other in eighteen years, but I heard that you were killed last year in a moped accident. Well, I happen to be in your neighborhood—I'm dead too—and I was just thinking that if you had any free time one of these days, maybe we could get a drink together . . . It's up to you, this is my number, ciao. Ah, sorry about asking for your number. Here it's easy to get other people's numbers. Unfortunately though, the deceased almost always keep their cell phones turned off, and I'm not having a lot of luck; I tried to find you in your room, but you weren't on your bed, nor under it. I tried to find you at the spot on the asphalt where you first stopped living: you weren't there. Evidently you stopped waiting. I hope you'll hear this message and call me back.

My mother went on seeing the man.
I followed him to his office: he was a civil servant who worked for the city government. I followed him home: he was married and had a fat nine-year-old daughter and a wife with a down-turned mouth and a dead look in her eyes. Then there was a mangy dog and a mountain of unread books, perfect, uncreased parallelepipeds, their pages too intimate with one another, almost as if glued together, certainly never glimpsed by human eyes. His

apartment was furnished in bad taste, with framed prints of Tower Bridge and English taxis and crude paintings of Parisian boulevards. He watched Arnold Schwarzenegger movies on TV and used a lot of mouthwash. He loved sausages and computer magazines. He beat off in the shower every morning and chatted on Facebook every night. He'd bring my mother flowers. I'd steal them from the vase and take them to my grave to replace the withered ones. Then I'd go back home.

They'd left. I picked my mother's forest-green dress up off the chair. I went downstairs and walked through the closed door of the darkroom. Using the dress as a blanket, I lay down to sleep on the floor.

On the evening of February 2, Man brought over a rented DVD and a pizza.

She put the pizza down on the dining room table and went back to him, kissed him greedily, took him by the hand, smiled; we all went into my mother's room. They undressed. The lights were off except for the sand-yellow Japanese table lamp on the nightstand. They kissed, they eyed each other, they licked each other, they started moving, I lay down next to my mother. He was caressing her breasts, he bent over her, over her thighs. She started panting. She spread her legs; I spread my legs.

02/05/2012, midnight: I feel so sorry for my body. I'm sorry that I failed to show it sufficient gratitude, when there was still time. I'd like to thank it for the tremendous wars it waged on viruses, the perfection of hunger and pain. I'd like to, but it's too late.

I slashed our veins, and now they no longer belong to anyone. They say that in the last instants of life a suicide always changes her mind, but this indecision actually continues even in death. The people who go to the cemetery to visit their loved ones would laugh at their own grief if they had any idea how much greater the grief of their loved ones is.

On February 11, 2012, Whitney Houston died, apparently from a mix of alcohol and antidepressants, and my boss yammered on about it all day.

Suddenly in his eyes she'd become an extraordinary artist. Facebook was full of her videos, accompanied by the commentary of weeping emoticons. The undying love that she proclaimed at the top of her lungs in her most famous song had spread like a virus through the entire online community. Everyone will always love her, even those who had never listened to her. Even new fathers and new mothers, obsessed with the canine grimaces of their children in pictures, had moved on from those photos to pictures of Whitney.

I tried to distract myself by arranging the new silver Bic pens on the shelf, but it was impossible: my boss kept commenting on videos and reading his comments aloud: "Another great talent destroyed by drugs. RIP Whitney."

It was unacceptable that death should perform this kind of facelift on the reputations of artists. It was equally unacceptable that, in contrast, death should have failed to perform any cosmetic surgery whatsoever on my identity: I was still the same behind-on-her-exams university student, and as if that weren't enough—now that eternity had entered the picture—being behind had taken on an insurmountable cosmic dimension.

I thought these things while lying in bed that night. And suddenly, in the hollow depths of myself, I found a tattered scrap of hope: a malingerer. A still-alive fish on the beach. A technological object that had once been useful but which was now overly complex and obsolete. I didn't know what to do with it, with hope. Suddenly, I sensed that something could change. But what?

I got up as if I were suffering from insomnia.

Right in front of my window was my dark wooden desk, with a black metal reading lamp and a pile of university textbooks. There were creased pamphlets from museum shows I'd never attended and discount coupons from perfume shops on Via Etnea. There were bus tickets I didn't need anymore. And Post-its with phone numbers written on them, samples of revitalizing conditioner and moisturizing creams, a hair band. A silver-plated frame with a picture of Lorenzo and me; what was that still doing there?

We were in the elevator, on our way up to the apartment we would live in together. Smiling. We had the strange proportions you always get in a selfie: my arm, holding the camera, was enormous and his head, behind mine, was too small. We looked like two snakes of different species put in the same glass cage by accident at the zoo. Happy in different ways, unaware of all the skin we'd have to shed. How could I have ever fallen in love with a guy like that, with a gym membership and a subscription to the "Star Wars" forum? Did I have to abandon my body underground in order to understand that this was all we had in common, that we belonged to the only human species to have survived for evolutionary reasons?

I flung the photo to the floor. I didn't bother picking up the shards because, after all, they can't hurt me anymore.

The sun was almost up. I rushed out as fast as I could go.

When I got to the end of Corso Italia I went down to the water. There was practically no one around, living or dead.

And I . . . will always . . . love youuu!

Whitney Houston's best-known song, which I'd never liked and which I now liked even less, bombarded my head. What a tasteless joke, to have a voice in my head telling me that it loves me.

Especially because that song, like all other songs, isn't for me anymore.

I knelt before the sea. Where the edge of the waves, never

cold, never damp, began. I knelt there as if facing a horizontal wall. A wall that runs from one blue to another, but each blue is more argumentative than the one before, it never lets me drown, it doesn't give me even a hint of goose bumps, a single miserable drop on my calves. *And I will always love you.*

I pulled out my leather diary. I decided that it was a letter for someone who would rescue me. And that someone is you.

The next Friday, when I got home from work, my mother wasn't there. I couldn't find her in her bedroom or any other room. I sat in my usual chair at the dining room table, waiting for her, until dawn. I waited for her until sunset. Then night again. Then dawn again. Then the afternoon. Then she came home.

She was with the man.

She threw her coat on the floor, her keys on the table by the door. She went into the bathroom and called: "Will you make the pasta? The pot's in the bottom right cabinet."

I opened the cabinet door and bent down; he reached through my fingers and grabbed the pot out of my hands. He filled it with water. My mother came back and said: "I have to go out and get some tomato sauce, I forgot that we don't have any." And she left.

I watched the water as it heated up. I watched my hands slide into it. I didn't have nerves anymore to tell me the excessive heat, nor did I have muscles to jerk my fingers out of the water. I didn't have anything but my monstrous freedom.

I was like the bacteria that were eating away at my body: invisible to the human eye, devoid of a nervous system to take care of me, but still perfectly capable of destruction. The man came over to check on the water. Little bubbles were stirring on the surface. I lifted the pot and dumped the water onto his face.

He screamed and threw himself to the floor.

My mother came back: "Oh my God, what happened? Carlo?"

"Help me! Help me! It burns! It burns!"

He was sobbing. He was shaking. The pot was on the floor. I went back to the front door and carefully hung up my mother's coat.

At the hospital they said that Man had second-degree burns.

Flat on his back in a white bed, he was grimacing, twisting the naked pulp of his face: he kept swearing that someone had thrown the water onto him. My mother smiled: "You're a little mixed up, try to get some sleep, you've been working so hard lately, and then you're having all those problems with your wife . . ."

Next to him in the bed were two people. There was an old man whose eyes were closed and whose arm was bandaged with a thousand tubes hanging off of his flesh, his chest rising and falling. Next to him, an old woman sobbed and sobbed; her chest was motionless and her arms were hooked to his chest.

She asked me: *"What's your name?"*

"You can see me?"

"Of course I can. I'm dead. Let's talk a little, please."

I left the room and wandered through the corridors of the burn unit. They were packed. Live moving bodies hobbling along, opening up manhole-smiles in the direction of passing white doctors, begging for good news. Tumbledown moving bodies, bodies with arms and legs bandaged like papier-mâché. Lumbering heavy bodies, damp, full of fluids and blotches and questions. Bodies jammed in among other bodies, lighter bodies: dead bodies.

Lots and lots of dead people, motionless, sitting or lying on the floor. They weren't bandaged, their flesh was disrupted, oozing rivers of pus, their faces and arms covered with flimsy white membranes, like jellyfish melting in the sun. There was a boy missing an arm who said to me: *"Sit down by me for a moment. Please."*

There was a little girl with no lips: *"I'm afraid."*

There was another girl in the corner: *"Tell me a story with a happy ending."*

There was a mother with her arms wrapped around her child and neither had a face, nothing but a bow of naked muscles. There were two blond twins, their chests riddled with holes; both boys were staring at me but I refused to see them. They looked at me and I closed my eyes. Cut it out, I'm not like you! At last my mother came out and we went home.

Hi, I'm Dorotea Giglio (1986–2011). You don't know me, but I remember your face. I saw it in the paper when you were killed. It was an accident: you happened to be crossing the street during a Mafia shootout. In the grainy photograph that appeared in the crime section, your face looked as untroubled as if you expected to live forever.

I'd like to get together and chat with you, find out how you're spending your eternal life, what new hobbies you've come up with for yourself, that kind of thing. Do you still go by the street where you died? Or does that stir unpleasant emotions for you? I died in the bathroom at home, and I wish going back there freaked me out and scared me. But every morning I still brush my teeth and shower in there. I use a cleansing cream for sensitive skin, I spend five minutes inspecting for blackheads, but I've stopped getting them. I still keep my makeup arranged on the shelf, first the dark lipsticks then the light ones then the mascara, and finally the makeup-removing wipes. As soon as I'm done with something I put it back where it belongs. I so wish that the fact that I'm dead would stir something in me: sadness, disgust, the desire to be elsewhere.

Man never came back to our apartment. I ran into him a couple of times at the supermarket, with a bandaged face. I saw him at his home, where I'd gone to get the striped tie my mother had given him and the photo of the two of them embracing with big smiles on the rocks of San Giovanni Li Cuti. I threw both the tie and the photo away.

2013

03/12/2013: My fibrous tissues have been reduced to shreds.
03/13/2013: My body is a threadbare overcoat.
03/14/2013, 6:00 P.M.: I'm happy, in spite of everything, to
still be able to be close to my body. It's not something every-
one could do. It takes affection, understanding, and plenty of
amour propre, alias necrophilia. There are times when I'd
like to steal all its bones. Wear them myself, as I did when
that was still my right. Do it while there's still time, before
they disappear. They're still as white and luminous as pearls.
When I was alive, I preferred pearls, but they never did any-
thing for me. My bones, on the other hand, supported me as
long as they could.

That night I went with Anna and Euridice to lie on the
beach and look at the sky. There were also a couple of little
kids who had died recently. When Anna was alive, she'd been
a dreamer. Now that she could only be dreamed, she was having a very hard time of things.

She said: *"I was religious, not a dreamer. It's different."*

She said: *"Just a few more months. We'll rise again before the*
end of the year."

We believed her. Our days were one long stag party: *"Aren't*
you excited that soon we'll be back together?" I kept asking my
body.

We waited.

We waited on Via Etnea, in front of the evergreen traffic

lights: when will the red light finally bloom? We waited outside the little beach houses at the Scogliera, outside the doors that opened onto lawns cared for by those who no longer cared about us. We waited outside the gates of the Villa Bellini, including the ones that were always open, but only to those of us who had moved past the body phase. Looking down at our own bodies, abandoned one after another underground as soon as their expiration dates passed. Looking down at our eyes, closed for mourning. Looking down at our brains: broken-down machines, soon to be junked. Looking down at our hearts: now fallen silent. Looking out at the sea, especially. One was a cross-eyed little girl with black hair and a sky-blue dress. She had died of brain cancer.

"Last night I dreamed about my Barbies again, the one with the camper and the one who's getting married. They were on my bed and they were chewing off each other's arms and legs. I don't want to be eaten, go tell the worms, please."

She was holding another little child in her arms, small and translucent like a rubber doll: it was only a fetus. No bigger than a raspberry, it had tiny fingers joined together and a vestigial tail. It had neither eyelids nor defined genitalia. The little girl had dressed it in the pink-and-white dress of her favorite doll, the blonde one with the closed mouth.

The sun started to set.

"Hush, children. That's the sun, it won't hurt you."

The little girl held the fetus up so it could get a better view of the amazing drop.

With death you forget so much, and you only learn a few new things, and all they do is befoul the wait. Now all we know how to do is wait. That's our only talent. We wait and we talk, we talk and we wait to talk. We do it lying down on the sea, most of all, but I also spend time at the cemetery: I'm a girl who likes to keep both feet on the ground. Waiting is one long meal, a cannibalism. We consume time just as time consumes our bodies underground. I like waiting; what else could I do, after all, now that no one waits for me anymore.

We prick up our ears, but there's nothing to be heard. We stretch our muscles, but there's nowhere they can take us. We hold out our fingers, but nothing ever allows itself to be grasped. The girl, squatting down on the ground, made a bridge with her chubby little finger for a ladybug to climb across, but the ladybug just walked right through it.

The little girl had a book, but we don't know how to read. So we started talking about the fetus: Was it born dead or did it die born? Is it on our team or on the team of the living?

Anna and a junkie riddled with track marks started playing catch with the fetus: as night fell, the little creature was an iridescent mist that flew from one pair of hands to the other. Euridice grabbed it and clutched it to her chest. She knotted the umbilical cord around her neck like a necklace.

I said, *"Stop playing with him! He's better than us!"*

"But it's fun! What a pill you are."

Anna opened her Bible. Euridice sat cross-legged and wrote. Her long, low-cut orange cotton dress, open wide to the clear blue sea, was like the sun bursting into a lens. Anna chose the passage. She doesn't know how to read either, but of all of us she has the most powerful memory.

"Awake and sing, ye that dwell in dust: for thy dew is as the dew of herbs, and the earth shall cast out the dead. Isaiah 26:19."

"But when? When will we rise again? When will I be able to go wake up my body underground? It's already mid-March!" says the little girl.

"Sooner or later," I reply. *"You just have to wait."*

"But does it know when to wake up?" asks the little girl.

"The body knows everything, don't you remember? Hot and cold, sleepiness . . ."

"No, I don't remember."

She grips my hand. The fetus is curled up on the ground on

a seashell: Botticelli's aborted Venus. The darkness is complete. The lights of the traffic and the bars are behind us: we can't see them, and they can't see us. The living are behind us: we can't see them, and they can't see us. Will the world really begin again? People keep coming over to our side, and so far we haven't seen anyone make the journey in the opposite direction. We wait. And we wait. And we wait. A one-way journey is for dreamers, lovers, lunatics.

Not for people like us. We wait for the return journey, the counterclockwise direction. We believe in Lazarus and Frankenstein, in Romero's zombies. We believe in Poe's Ligeia, who comes back more beautiful than before. Faith is important: faith in God, faith in Stephen King, faith in *Ghost Whisperer*. Our faith has been cleansed of terror and of guilt. We're not frightened of Christ's cross nor of Buffy's. Faith is the imaginary ring on Carrie's fingers as they reach out of the grave.

I wait. I wait as if inside a defused bomb. I wait to have weight. I wait stretched out underneath the grass of the cemetery, holding my hand, as if to tell my body that the worst is over. Or else on the lawn, my head on the wet grass, my eyes wide open. *For thy dew is as the dew of herbs, and the earth shall cast out the dead.* I wait, but deep in my chest my heart no longer keeps count. One, two, three . . . Green light? No, the light is still red. I wait. On my wrist, instead of a watch, I have an oracle: the cuts on my veins are motionless minute and hour hands. This is the memento mori of my eternity: time is broken, don't cry, it's stopped bleeding.

I never saw that little girl again: as we say in Italian, if you don't die, we'll see you another time. If you do die, on the other hand, we'll almost never see you again, and certainly no one will miss you.

The fetus, on the other hand, I took home with me.

First I hung him up by its arms on the coatrack, next to the leather jacket. Then I gave him a name, Geremia, after the prophet Jeremiah, and I put him on my bed with my stuffed animals: he was the sweetest one, after the blue elephant that my mother gave me for my fourth birthday.

Then I started taking him out on a leash up and down Corso Italia. Every now and then the deceased would stop and pet him, asking me how many months he'd been dead and that sort of thing.

On Saturday, October 8, outside the Geox store, a guy around thirty with intelligent green eyes told me I looked like Lily Collins, and that Geremia looked like the floating fetus attached to Frida Kahlo's womb in her famous painting.

I really liked Kahlo but I hoped that Geremia wasn't one of her aborted children, for his sake; that way he wouldn't have to suffer the regret of painterly qualities lost even before he'd had a chance to inherit them. Lily Collins, however, was new to me: I had to ask my boss, who knows how to read, to look her up. She's the daughter of the singer Phil Collins, she played Snow White in the movie *Mirror Mirror* a year after my death.

That night on YouTube I watched her flail around for hours, a smile on her face and a crown on her head, wearing a yellow-and-blue dress made by Eiko Ishioka: she was singing "I Believe in Love" and she repeated it over and over again, ad infinitum. Eiko Ishioka died of pancreatic cancer not long after the movie came out.

The next day I waited outside Geox, hoping to see him again. The young man didn't come back. Same thing the next day.

At two in the morning I clicked PLAY again, to fall asleep: luckily Lily Collins, surrounded by gilded walls, under a camera rising straight up to God, still believed in love.

I never saw the young man with intelligent green eyes again.

I continued to take Geremia on long walks, after work. Since he never spoke or moved, I didn't know if he liked me, but I knew he was better than I was, because he'd never been human.

Sometimes we'd go for walks at night, when there wasn't a living soul around. Anna would follow me, dragging her feet. She'd say: *"I'm tired."*

She'd say: *"The earth mourneth and fadeth away, the world languisheth and fadeth away, the haughty people of the earth do languish. The earth also is defiled under the inhabitants thereof; because they have transgressed the laws, changed the ordinance, broken the everlasting covenant. Therefore hath the curse devoured the earth, and they that dwell therein are desolate: therefore the inhabitants of the earth are burned, and few men left. Isaiah 24:4-6."*

We walked along Viale Ionio, night after night. Geremia would drag along in the dust like a dead dog, but other times I'd carry him in my arms. Anna would say: *"I'm tired."*

Walking through those dark streets at night, I hoped that one day I'd see my father and that he'd be dead. Without a body to abandon me with, perhaps this time he'd stay with me.

04/19/2013, noon: The aerobic germs have excavated a monstrous place for themselves deep inside my body. They've taken up residence in cabins made of disintegrating tissues.
5 P.M.: My bones are ramshackle windows that look out on nothing; my skin is so many tattered curtains.
5:09 P.M.: With no more barriers between the world and my soul, thousands of germs and beetles enter and exit my body. Thousands of germs and beetles have become Dorotea Giglio. Now, in the tumbledown castle of flesh I once called "me," I'm a complete stranger.

I'm Dorotea Giglio (1986–2011), your niece. I don't know your cell number, so I'm speaking to you from the banks of the river where you drowned. I just wanted to ask you something: where are you?

I'd really like to get to know you. I'd like for us to become friends. When I was little I dreamed about you all the time. Actually I dreamed about a jar in which I felt I was suffocating. Was that how you felt too, while you were drowning? I know which bed was yours in the house in Trecastagni and I know what chair you sat in at the dinner table. I know which glass was yours, and which cup. But you don't sit in that chair anymore. I've seen plenty of people stay seated in their chairs, you know. Everyone has a chair of their own, a building of their own, a stretch of roadside of their own, right before where the car hit them. I have a bathtub, but now it's full of insects. Where are you?

The man never came back, and Aunt Clara started coming over every day again, the way she had right after I died. They resumed that silence of theirs too, that way they had of dining together with pat phrases until they locked eyes by accident, and then they'd fall silent. It was May 12, 2013, and it was raining out. My mother was talking about an Iranian film she'd seen in the theater; she reached for the pepper without looking up. Aunt Clara talked about the latest titles from her publishing house: "Do you want me to bring you that French grammar textbook with the updated 2013 edition of the dictionary?"

She hadn't looked up.

"No, no, thanks, forget about it."

My mother didn't look at her either.

It was more than I could stand.

I stood up.

They no longer had reason to avoid each other's gaze for fear of seeing Lidia's eyes. Now those were my eyes, not theirs, the certified copies of Lidia's eyes. Underground those eyes had filled up with blasphemous larvae, ready to suck my entire soul out through my scleras. The irises had lost their color, the sockets had become imprints of forgotten dry riverbeds. Now, with my retinas caved in, without the blankets of my eyelids, I was naked as never before. Now Lidia and I—her body buried who knows where—certainly resembled each other. Identical and similarly alone in the uniform of our bones, we had twin eyes. Four empty holes, like the nail holes in the wall of the villa in Trecastagni. Like the four chipped pale-pink bowls that you used for breakfast, Greta-Clara-Lidia-mother, withered little family, and now in that house, on the highest kitchen shelf, they're stitched together by a spiderweb.

My mother gradually resumed the life she led before I died.

In the summer she'd go stay with Aunt Clara in Costa Saracena and she'd water plants on the balcony dressed in white. In the winter she'd turn on the radiators. All year round she'd wash her undergarments and remember not to leave the milk out of the fridge. She started to use insecticide, so the house emptied of insects, but I stayed, I continued to stand by her, to eat lunch and dinner with her, but without sleeping in her bed, so as not to frighten her.

08/28/2013: The ligaments are broken. The cartilage is breaking.
08/29/2013: My mouth is nothing more than a crack in the wall. Silence.

2014

Time passed.

I went on dining with my mother and my aunt, I went on giving my mother goodnight kisses. In the morning I'd lie on the bed while she made it, letting cotton and air pass through me. At night I'd come home from work before she did, I'd wait for her at the door, and when she walked in and dropped her jacket on the floor I'd hang it up on the coatrack. I'd sit on the sofa with her and Clara while they watched TV at night, and when they went to bed I'd put the remote control back on the coffee table and straighten the cushions, turn out the halogen lamp and the light in the hall.

On June 29, deep in the earth, my connective tissues had all crumbled to pieces. That evening Aunt Clara called my mother from her office.

She was pregnant.

"How can you not know who the father is?"

My mother talked with her, stretched out on her bed. I sat next to her, and I laughed and laughed and laughed.

Time passed.

Now it was my mother who cooked for Clara, who was more and more pregnant all the time, swollen and awkward, but with the expression of a generous mammal. She even seemed happy.

I'd never be happy.

In your posthumous years, at a certain point, you arrive at what at first might be taken for pessimism, but it's really the malady of objectivity. Objectivity is the malady of things as they are. Objectivity has a sudden onset, a collateral effect of the suspension of one's encephalic functions. It shows up uncooked and intact, with neither an instruction booklet nor a definite article.

Objectivity is a rough timber, and it's up to you to light the fire, with your senses. I lost my senses along with my body. My senses have become elucubrations. Objectivity begins with my death. It begins in my body, where there are now more worms than there is identity, it begins and it increases, slowly, as the flesh vanishes and the bones corrode.

Objectivity is a fine object, multifunctional. It looks lovely in the middle of a room, so wide open and brightly lit. Its straight lines attract attention, its glow enchants. It's very useful, if combined with a working sensory apparatus. It can produce the lacerating sound of truth or the syncopated songs of science. But without a sensory apparatus, it's like a stereo without speakers.

Result: continual, incurable incomprehension, a long stay in the white hospital of eternity, without any hope of recovery. All around us life is teeming, but it reaches us only as a blocked idea, a congress of actions that will never bear fruit, unpaid rent on an apartment overlooking the past. It arrives as a glitter of scalpels without risks, and what meaning does it have?

Objectivity is the alphabet that doesn't come to us as bricks of phrases but as the naked debris of buildings, stones by the roadside. Let those who have truly loved life cast the first "a."

Time passed.

My tendons were all destroyed and my bones lost their protein component. The wrinkles closed around my mother's lips and the damp ate away at the living room ceiling. It rained all March and the stain on the ceiling turned darker and darker; underground my ligaments came loose from the bones; two diagonal creases extended under my mother's eyes. She had more and more white hair; my hair continued falling out. From her hands emerged the road maps of her veins and the hardness of her knuckles.

Time passed, my body rotted, but I grew no older. In the opaque mirror in the living room I saw a twenty-five-year-old girl, smooth-skinned, with freckles and clean, glistening hair. In the opaque mirror in the living room, for hours, I would dream of myself covered with lines, the way I never would be.

At night, with my eyes closed and my hands clasped, I'd pray: Dear God, give me varicose veins and missing teeth. Thinning intervertebral discs. Shrinking bones. I want to feel my cerebral mass recede and my spinal column shrink.

I dreamed of the old age I'd never have. I wanted to grow old with my mother, but obviously that would never happen. Time, the same time that was passionately dismantling my body underground, had seduced me and abandoned me. And I, like a voyeur, continued to spy on the passing hours. I stalked the days. Every morning in the mirror I'd search my skin: never a mark. I measured my hair with a ruler: always the same length.

This is why the calendar is a precious object. The months are postcards from some distant place, a sumptuous Middle Eastern city. Sitting on my bed, certain nights, I'd leaf through it like a forbidden book, lingering over the empty squares like pictures of gilded mosques. Then I'd put it back where it belonged, on its nail, opened to the month of July.

On January 5 something horrible happened.

I fell in love for the second time, the first time since I died.

His name was Alberto, but I'm not sure that matters much. Alberto was the new salesclerk in the stationery store where I work. Alberto like Albert, the officer loved by Victor Hugo's daughter, the one she followed to the ends of the earth while he continued to avoid her, all the way to Barbados, by which point she had lost her mind, and walked through the streets dressed in rags, past barefoot boys who threw stones at her, and when she finally saw him again she failed to recognize him. Alberto like my Lupo Alberto agenda from middle school. Alberto like all the times that I encounter something lovely and incomprehensible.

He came to work for us on January 5. That day Sinéad O'Connor attempted suicide.

They kept running clips of the video of "Nothing Compares 2 U" on the BBC: the close-up of her tear-streaked face, her walking in a black tunic past statues and through gardens. I've always loved Sinéad O'Connor in all her manifestations. When she tore up the picture of the pope. When she became a nun without taking a vow of chastity. When she wore a tank top and army boots with a shaved head and sang about phoenixes rising from the flames and dragons to be killed, and husbands lost on far shores and tears scattered on the beach. When she screamed about eternal music in Gaelic, and women lying on their lovers' graves. And then when silence fell on the dragons and phoenixes: she no longer sang then, she said that she was going to devote herself to her family and nothing else. She appeared on TV only rarely, twenty pounds heavier and with a weakened voice, she supported lawsuits against child molesters in the Irish church and hit sour notes while singing some of her best songs live. Then she'd tweeted about her sexual frustrations and placed a personal ad in the *Irish Independent* to find a boyfriend. She'd found an analyst and married him only to file for divorce after just eighteen days. Then this. She'd called the newsroom of *The Sun* to tell them that she'd tried to commit suicide by overdosing in London after the failure of this fourth marriage of hers. Why tell the press? If I'd survived I wouldn't have told anyone. But she'd even gone so far as to ask on Twitter whether anyone knew a method of suicide that would keep her children from figuring out that she'd done it on purpose. I was flabbergasted. I kept watching a YouTube video of that concert of hers in which she, still so skinny, slowly took off her clothes, from a black coat to a high-necked dress to a cat burglar's black leotard, singing: "I feel so different." It was the unveiled meaning of the striptease, performed to spite all the ridiculous Jennifer Lopezes on MTV. It was a free fall toward truth that came to a stop just short of her skeleton. "I feel so different." How beautiful her voice was, with that saturated, imploring rage of hers, how beautiful she was, so skinny, so close to the bone, wrapped in that leotard as if she were asking her bones: what next?

She'd told the press: "God obviously wants me around—though I can't think why." She'd announced a new CD, and had posed in a low-cut dress with a tattoo on her chest of Jesus in the middle of a cloud, wearing the crown of thorns, a huge bleeding heart in His hands. Sinéad had tried to kill herself but hadn't succeeded. I had. Between her and me, who had won, and who had lost?

Just then Alberto came in.

I looked up from the computer. He was so handsome: he had blue eyes and black hair and he was alive. Alberto was a very sad answer to my question.

Horoscope for the sign of Leo (for those who died between July 23 and August 22): The quadrature of Uranus no longer concerns you. Neptune returns to his house, but you aren't invited.

That same evening I hurried over to see my body and tell it that I had a crush on someone.

01/5/2015, 10:03 P.M.: Now my body is populated by fungi. They've colonized my decomposing brown fat. Fungi are one of the few things I know about my body's current life. I know that it has Aspergillus candidus.
11:59 P.M.: So depressing. There are times when I can't wait for it to turn into ashes, to put an end to this excruciating wait. There are times when I wish I could give my body a posthumous euthanasia, and spare it all the worms still to come.

Every morning at work I'd talk to Alberto.

I told him about my father, about my mother, about my problems, about Lorenzo, about Aunt Clara, about Lidia whom I'd never met, about our house in Trecastagni and about Clara's house in Costa Saracena, about the locked drawers containing the forbidden pictures of Lidia. I showed him a picture of me and Lorenzo on my cell phone and the cuts on my wrists.

"Yes, there are two extra cuts on the right wrist because I didn't do them right. It's hard to hit the center of the vein."

After I'd told him everything, I felt so good.

"Speak from the heart": when we were alive we used to say that, it meant to fill your words with feeling. To speak from the heart: we were first-rate ventriloquists, but now our puppet is rotting underground. To speak from the heart: now it's a dialogue, and the rotting heart doesn't reply.

At the cemetery I've seen plenty of dead people exhume their hearts. Their fingers reemerge filthy with mud, and they pin their rotten, lurid hearts to their flesh like a brooch. But it's only a masquerade. They'll be found out. Maybe not today, maybe not tomorrow, but one day emotion will burst out all over them like a popping zit: obscene, liquid, a mass of dense filaments that will pour out of the decomposing heart and down their bodies.

The dead person will try to put all the parts back together, to clean things up, but the heart will be everywhere, ejaculating a disorderly meshwork of pus and blood, ramified veins and empty tubes, pustules swollen like closed eyes, lesions like open mouths, excrescences as porous as tongues. In the explosion, his feelings will have left a single motionless fragment on his chest. That point, immobile and solid as a nail, is the nail of objectivity. It's the only truth available. You can hang all the emotions on it that you want, they'll just flake off like scabs from a wound.

You can hate it all you like, the nail of objectivity, but it's our nail, our lurid personal baggage, like the shopping carts that the homeless push around. It's our fake ID, the way we remain among the living without meeting any of the requirements. And because it's ours, we must respect it and take good care of it.

It was wonderful to talk with Alberto. We had the same tastes: Michel Gondry, Naomi Watts, frozen yogurt. We ate some together a couple of times, after work, at the cart in Piazza Stesicoro. He liked horror movies okay too: *The Evil Dead, The Thing, The Others, Poltergeist.* I wish that I could still enjoy them for the adrenaline rush, and not just for the clumsiness of the plot.

The Thursday after that, our boss asked Alberto to lock up, but I stayed behind to keep him company. Then at eight o'clock the phone rang: "Yes, sweetheart, right away. I'll be at your place at nine. Love you."

He left; it was dark out the way it ought to be. The wind blew. Alberto had a girlfriend and he was going to swing by and pick her up at nine. He got into his blue Fiat Panda. I stayed there for a while, motionless, trying to remember what it feels like when someone's coming to pick you up at nine. I sat motionless for half an hour, five inches above the sidewalk. I stared at the empty rectangle with the blue outlines where just a short time before Alberto's car had been parked. A kid went by with earbuds and yellow highlights in his hair; he wasn't much to look at. No doubt he too had a date later that evening at a specific time. For an instant, just as he walked past me, I was tempted to throw myself at his feet and beg him to make a trade: please, please, all my eternity in exchange for your 9 P.M.

The period of my crush on Alberto coincided with my ammoniacal phase.

Inside me, along with love, ammonia developed, and a vast swarm of larvae took up residence in my interior. Among them were plenty of flies but also beetles of the species *Nicrophorus humator*. While I was busy trying to make Alberto fall in love with me, they were busy scrubbing me clean of the black ooze that drenched me.

At night, in bed, while my mother watched documentaries on the La7 network, I thought about Alberto: about the white gown I'd wear for our wedding, and about my body, even whiter, once it had emerged entirely from the filth of the tissues. Purified, geometric, honest, a jewel of precious bones. And my eyes: emptied of cornea and of gaze, naked sockets like stone windows in a castle, so that the soul, instead of being reflected in them, would finally reveal itself whole, all its love looking out, no longer inverted, finally true.

Horoscope for the sign of Leo (for those who died between July 23 and August 22): Saturn continues to reside in Libra, but don't go visit him, he's not expecting you.

Now that Sinéad O'Connor had attempted suicide, I looked at her poster over my bed with new eyes: like an expensive dress in a shop window, with guilty yearning. I wanted her all for myself, in my network of friends, in my death: I called to her, as if out of malice, but I was just incurably dead. It had never occurred to me that I might wish for someone else's death. Before, it would have been wickedness, not loneliness.

Geremia was stretched out on the ground, in the dust, like a Muslim prayer rug.

Since he died in utero, his body underwent maceration, meaning that the decomposition of his flesh, protected from extrinsic factors and microbes, took place solely through internal agents. No worm had ever touched his body. It's truly fascinating. It's the highest degree of self-sufficiency. His entire annihilation is a personal matter, pure introspection. I admired his independence: when he grew up he would have been a strong man, sufficient unto himself; he would have dispensed unconditional love without any selfish desire to receive love in exchange.

On January 12, I went with Alberto to the wine store near the stationery shop to buy a bottle of Nero d'Avola, my favorite. His girlfriend came with us. We went to get a pistachio gelato on Corso Italia. I liked him so much that when I was near him I lacked air. I felt the lack of the six liters of oxygen that I took into my lungs every minute when I was alive.

On January 15 he gave me a scarf. It used to belong to his girlfriend. I stroked it all day long. I hurried to pay myself a visit.

Having a scarf around my neck unleashed all sorts of absurd thoughts in me. Like for instance: being cold, being hot, the feeling of the wool. The whole way to the cemetery I played at putting it on and taking it off, imagining that it made me feel warmer or colder. I got to the headstone. I wrapped the scarf around my body's neck.

01/15/2015, 10:00 P.M.: I love Alberto in a way that's different from how I loved Lorenzo. It's strictly a physical thing. The beat of my heart is no longer the twofold closure of the two atrioventricular valves followed by the closure of the aortic and pulmonary valves. My skin no longer encloses my body and my sternum no longer encloses my heart. Now I'm wide open, around the clock. Open to worms, open to bacteria. Now I'm wide open like a house with broken windows. The vessels of my arteries, underground, are now flowerpots for all creation. My heart is thrown open to external agents, under the soil trodden by one and all. From Lorenzo's doormat I've graduated to being the doormat of the whole universe, and it's much nicer and much fairer. It's unconditional love.

When I got home I was in an excellent mood. I caught up with my mother in the kitchen and I broke the truth to her: *"Your apartment is infested, I'm sorry."*

01/16/2015: Beetles defecate on every tendon.
01/17/2015: Horrible little butterflies attack my flesh. A lurid dust starts from my skull: yes, that really was once my hair.

On January 18—it was a Sunday—I went up Mount Etna with Alberto, Sara, Anna, and Euridice. We walked on the snow-covered dirt path, surrounded by black birches. The footsteps of the two living people made noise. We reached the lava-stone cave of the Bocche di Fuoco. Sara sat down in the cave and got out the sandwiches. She said that it was too cold, she complained, she rubbed her arms against her chest. Anna and Euridice remained standing, amid the dark shadows, crossing their arms over their chests the way Sara had done.

Anna trembled and said slowly: *"I'm cold."*

Euridice trembled and said slowly: *"I'm hungry, I'm thirsty, I'm sleepy."*

Alberto emerged from the cave and went to get water from the cistern at one of the huts. I followed him, walked with him, behind him.

At Canova Park, in Australia, in 1979, Mary D. Leakey found a set of footprints. They belonged to a man and a woman, two Australopithecines, who were running away from a fire in search of safety in a clearing. I don't remember where I read it, but I do remember that it's the oldest documented escape.

01/18/2015: Nicrophorus humator, *I don't hold it against you, I know that you need my flesh, but do you need it as much as I do?*

On January 19 it was drizzling out. It was almost closing time. Alberto was organizing the discounted 2015 agendas.

"I realize we haven't known each other long, but I have this urge to tell you everything, you know."

He put on his overcoat.

"And I mean everything. I hope that's okay with you."

He said goodnight to our boss. He went out. He opened his umbrella. I followed him to his car. We had ten minutes at our disposal: that's how long it usually took him to get home. He fastened his seat belt and checked his rearview mirror. He started the engine.

"When I was nine years old my mother started spending too much time in the bathtub. This is something I've never told anyone else. Before taking her bath she'd set the dinner table with our Christmas tablecloth and light a white candle at the center of the table. I don't know why. She'd lay out the red porcelain dishes that my grandmother had bought her in Holland. Those dishes are gone now, because my mother smashed them all against the wall when I was, like, eleven, one night when she was completely drunk. Anyway, whenever I saw the table set, I knew that she was in the bath and that she'd be in there a long time. I'd sit down at the table, in my designated chair, and watch the candle burn down. I'd clutch Lidia's broken teddy bear to my chest. I was terrified, my heart was racing furiously."

Alberto braked at the stop sign. He rolled down the window.

"If by the time the candle had burned down and gone out my mother still hadn't emerged from the bathroom, I would run in terror to check on her."

Alberto lit a cigarette.

"At first I'd call out or knock hard on the door, but she never answered. I'd put my ear to the door and concentrate."

Alberto put the car back in gear and pulled out.

"As soon as I heard anything, even the slightest movement, I'd heave a sigh of relief. She's still alive, I'd tell myself. She's still alive."

Alberto turned on the radio.

By January 21 my hair had all fallen out, scattered around my skull. On January 21 I touched Alberto's hair.

It was raining, he got to work late, as he came in he said: "I'm drenched." I took advantage of the opportunity to reach out and touch his hair. I said: *"It's true, I'll run and get you the hair dryer, I have a portable one that I keep in the back."*

His hair was as soft and sweet-smelling as gold.

I wasn't certain that gold was soft and sweet-smelling. Plus, his hair was black. It was black because it was the same color as the panthers in the documentary that my mother was watching the day before, and that same night Euridice told me that panthers are black. She is an archeologist of the senses: even though she no longer has them, she's memorized them better than the rest of us. She remembers one hundred percent. She can look inside herself without crashing into her organs. She smiles and her smiles speak the interior instead of imitating the exterior the way ours do.

I left Euridice sitting on the saltwater with her notebook and went to the zoo to touch a panther. At first I was too scared to go into the cage: useless inhibitions from when I was alive. The panther was sleeping. I extended a trembling hand toward it.

I pulled the hand back.

I couldn't touch it. But there was no doubt about it: the panther was black in the same way that Alberto's hair was. I left with the same sense of satisfaction I felt in middle school when I solved an equation. The panther was black and beautiful; Alberto's hair was black and beautiful.

But why was the panther black while Alberto had black hair? Did the fact that the panther identified with its black while Alberto didn't identify with his make the black of one different from that of the other?

I came to a halt, discouraged, in the deserted street.

I was no longer sure that anything about the panther's appearance could help me understand Alberto's hair. I wasn't sure that there was anything in the world capable of bringing me any closer to understanding him, and without understanding him, I had no chance of being loved in return.

Because after all colors don't exist. They are simply our way of codifying the intensity of light, and they came about strictly for evolutionary reasons: our ancestors needed to distinguish between one fruit and another in the forest. Now that I no longer needed to evolve, now that I had been dismissed from civilization, the falsehood of colors revealed itself to me in all its ignominy. How could I ever hope to conquer Alberto, if we weren't victims of the same lies?

I passed through the street door of my apartment building.

My mother was still up and was watching a documentary about the Second World War with Clara. If I had sat down beside them, neither one would have had to move over. I wasn't even capable of reducing the amount of space available.

I withdrew into my room. Not my room from when I was alive, the room of my death. The room of my death is the entire universe, and I occupy no more than a little corner of it at the cemetery, out of shyness. When I reached the dark cemetery, I followed the path that led to my remains: by now I knew the way by heart, I no longer needed any light. Two dogs could be heard conversing in melancholy tones on distant balconies, along with the siren of an ambulance, quickly swallowed up in silence.

I arrived at my headstone.

I lay down.

I took the dry grass between my fingers. Soft? Smooth? Hard? And what color? In the dark I'm justified in not knowing. I yanked out the blades of grass one by one, grinding my teeth. *"This is the real world,"* I said to myself, *"and it's not here for you."*

01/22/2015: All the cartilage has crumbled.
01/23/2015: The flesh that remains is just thin leather. Arsenic runs through the remaining hair, but there's no one left to poison.
01/24/2015: Soon I'll be nothing but calcium carbonate and calcium phosphate. A chemical formula.

For my fourth birthday since my death, January 30, Euridice arranged a wonderful surprise for me. She had me meet her at the beach and there she handed me two plane tickets to London:

"I understand how you feel, dead for just a few years, it's depressing, I've been through it myself."

The tickets were used bus tickets, because of course we didn't need real tickets, since we were invisible. Just as we had no need for reservations for the five fabulous nights in whatever five-star hotel we might choose. We would get drunk for free on all the alcohol we wanted to take from the minibar. And, best of all, we were going to see Amy Winehouse in concert.

Euridice really helped me a lot. I'd never had her initiative and willpower, but then she never had my twenty-five years of age. There's always a reason to envy other dead people. A more intact skeleton, fewer insects at the corner of the mouth, or a nicer past. More people at your funeral, more chrysanthemums around your headstone, less fading in the letters that make up your name. Now that we're all stagnating in the bottom half of the hourglass, with no more time at our disposal, our past is the diamond that we wear every day, jealously. We always want ours to be the one that glitters the brightest.

Like greedy thieves we ask the others what they did for a living, whether they had children, if they achieved their dreams, and with every good memory we'd like to plunge our hands right into them and steal it. Were you famous? How many people did you have sex with? The questions can get very cynical: how many people did you have under you? Now that we're under everyone, in the foul belly of the earth, that's an important question.

I don't have Euridice's initiative. I don't have her self-confidence, and my self is lost forever. Still, what do I care about being the best, now that my identity is no longer a valid currency in the world? The past is a diamond that we wear every day. Every one of its facets is different but every facet reenacts the last instant of life. Every facet of my diamond is as cold and white as a bathtub.

The Royal Albert Hall was a labyrinth full of gilt friezes and stairways upholstered in velvet, too many entrances and too many exits, too many coat checks, too many dead blonde English girls directing you to the correct row. We found our seats. Amy Winehouse came onstage almost immediately, alone, without applause and without musicians. It was dark; she stood at center stage with her skinny legs, her black eyes, a skimpy little yellow dress that fell above her knees, and six-inch crocodile high heels. She swayed, she set down an empty glass and grabbed the mike, then she smiled. Her hair was piled high in her usual teased sixties-style beehive, and out of the middle of it stuck little cloth bees on metal wires. The audience clapped at the pun.

The meaning was clear. In English, her hairdo was called a beehive, and so Amy had simply added the bees. It's pretty simple. We can no longer chat with our parents, sweethearts, neighbors, grandparents, children, siblings, friends. Now that the living can no longer hear us, our words remain inside us, raw and misshapen, like steaks gone bad. We turn them over on our tongues, tirelessly, our carrion-words, until we finally make puns of them: that's all we can do. Rhymes, alliterations—what else can we do with them? It's a sad and moving game. Now that the alphabet has gone bad and words no longer communicate anything, we love making them communicate with each other. It's a little bit like playing with Barbie dolls: a regression to childhood, something that begins in old age, and after death goes on and on and on.

Amy grabbed the microphone.

"Hi, everyone. I'm glad you're here. Don't feel sorry for me, my intestine's as empty as a crystal vase, the alcohol that killed me ensures that it doesn't fill up with anaerobic bacteria."

She started singing. She was strange and wonderful. Her octaves followed scales that weren't the traditional musical scales. They were spiral staircases, twisting in ever narrower and tighter coils, suspended in midair.

I had imagined that people's voices changed once they were dead. But dead Amy's voice was more like Amy's voice than it had been when she was alive. It was a sound as identical to itself as a memory: distant, vague, circular, it kept coming back to itself like a carousel. It was a déjà-vu voice, it was in our heads. Amy sang in playback and each one of us was the memory of her voice. In the middle of her best song, while she was saying, *"And I go back to,"* she fell to the floor. I would have gone to help her, but I know that you can't die twice. Amy wasn't moving. Not even blinking.

The song went on.

Folded up on her side on the floor, skinny and limp as a long insect, eyes closed, one high heel shoe kicked off her foot, and a black sea of hair poured out onto the stage, she went on, without missing her high notes and without moving her lips. In the deserted and silent Royal Albert Hall, two living ushers slowly gathered up crumpled playbills and empty beers from under the seats. A dented water bottle. A cell phone. A straw. We listened to Amy. No one complained about the fact that her body was not performing along with her voice. No one seemed to miss the ritual of lips opening and closing in time with the song.

"Back to Black" ended.

"Thank you. Sorry I'm not in better shape, I'll come to soon enough, but first I'll sing another one for you. Where's my father? Daddy, are you there? Do you see my father in the audience? It doesn't matter, it doesn't matter, now I'll sing you one from my new album, I hope you like it. Daddy, this one's for you, I love you so much."

The lights went out. She started singing again in complete darkness. Lying there, motionless, eyes half shut. The theater was closed for the night.

That night we went to sleep in a five-star hotel on Oxford

Street. We walked through all the doors until we found an unoc-
cupied room. All night long, on the silk bedcovers, we talked.

I talked about Alberto.

Euridice told me about her unsuccessful career as a writer:
when she was alive she hadn't had time to publish and now she
couldn't remember what the point of publishing had been.

When she was alive, Euridice had been a cosmic pessimist,
but now that the cosmos was no longer her hotel—now that
she had checked out and was only touring the place, without
living in any of the rooms—the positive and negative aspects of
that place were no longer any of her business.

*01/28/2015: Freedom, so important for the living, becomes
unbelievably shabby the minute you die: reality can no longer
impose any limits on it. The same thing goes for freedom of
speech: no one can hear you. There's nothing sadder than an
excess of freedom. I'm lucky: I have a little less than the others, because I'm in love. That's a limit. A line. My one and
only line, a barbed wire that separates Alberto and me from
everything else.*

I was very happy to go back to work.

When we put prices on things, I'd always talk to Alberto.

I hoped that the fact that I was dead wouldn't be a problem.
Love demands a future, and I don't have one. What's done is
done. My everyday actions, my work and my friendships, my
walks all have a meaning that goes no further than itself; they
protect me from the boredom of eternity but they lead to nothing. What fascinated me about Alberto was that everything he
did, even eating, had repercussions on his life: the food made
his body rounder, movement tired him, the movies he saw made
him more cultured and added to his pleasure. Me, on the other
hand, they gave nothing; the images had turned stingy. It was
frustrating.

One time I sat down next to Alberto and his girlfriend, Sara.

She is prettier than me, she smells of life in progress, and her hair grows and grows and grows. When she looks at someone, that someone returns her look. When she speaks, people listen. Her hands communicate messages of cold and heat, depending on the outside temperature: her skin isn't a solitary and apathetic material, the way mine is. She has sufficient facial nerves to smile, and the nerve endings of her lips haven't yet ended.

All of these characteristics are very attractive in a human being; it was perfectly normal that Alberto should fall in love with a woman like her. How could I blame him?

I walked with them down Via Etnea. I walked with them as they held hands along the paths of the Villa Bellini. I sat with them in his blue Fiat when they went out to buy groceries. I followed them among the shelves, I laid my hand on the package of chocolate cookies that he'd picked up and put back. I laid my hand on the can of corn he'd brushed when he'd reached for the tuna. I stood in line with them at the cash register. I went home. To Alberto's home. I would sit with them at the table while they ate. I would sit with them on the little balcony while they read the paper and talked. I would sit on a chair, in the bedroom, while they fucked.

02/04/2015, 5:39 A.M.: Underground, my white bones hand over to the third group of fungi what remains of my flesh.

I left. I walked down Via Etnea. I reached Piazza Duomo. The parish priest of the cathedral basilica, dressed in purple, was presenting Saint Agatha's relics to her devoted followers.

I walked as far as Porta Uzeda.

There was lots of noise and movement. There was a cart on which stood the statue of Saint Agatha; she was covered with gold, with a white face and little eyes, and a glassy gaze. The cart struggled toward Piazza Cutelli; I followed it, crushed between the people, compressed in the knotted muscles, liquid amid their blood, intubated in their veins, tossed about between intestines and stomachs, bewildered, exhausted. I followed the cart along Via Vittorio Emanuele, then to Piazza dei Martiri, Via VI Aprile, Via della Libertà, Piazza Iolanda. I didn't know where I was going. The relics continued their journey. Via Umberto, Grotte Bianche, Piazza Carlo Alberto. Men in long white tunics supported the cart. Families with children and balloons, me tossed to and fro in the depths of their flesh and mixed up with the helium in the balloons. Shouts. Piazza Stesicoro. Stands selling candy apples and chunks of sugar coal and peppermint sticks. Stands selling pistachio crepes and granitas. Ice cream. Old men sitting on benches, children riding on their parents' shoulders, dogs with their tongues lolling out, and me in the midst of their saliva, the smog, the fumes of exhaust and ricotta, sweat, cotton candy, me liquid in the prosecco in every glass, in the bars lining the way up to the Salita dei Cappuccini, in the mouths that talked and talked, in the lips pressed together in a kiss, in the closed, dark lips. The statue made its way up the hill and reached Piazza San Domenico. At 8:07 P.M., the relics came to a halt at the Church of Sant'Agata la Vetere.

At 8:07 P.M., in my body, the *Dactylium fusaroides* never stop for a second.

At 8:07 P.M., the relics were greeted joyfully in the church.

At 8:07 P.M., there is no one to preserve what remains of me. Soon there will be nothing left of me, nothing left, nothing left. The *Verticillium candelabrum* have no idea of what they're doing to me.

I hurried to Alberto's apartment, I was exhausted, exhausted, I fell to my knees at the foot of his bed.

"I'll always be there for you."

Sara lay down on top of him. Sara, her hands, her legs, her mouth devouring him.

On my knees, I kept saying to him: *"I'll always be there for you."*

"I'll always be there for you."

"I'll always be there for you and I'll never hurt you, I'll never even lay a finger on you."

When I got to work the next day, my boss stood up.

"Do you want to tell me what the heck you're trying to do?"

"What, excuse me?"

"You know perfectly well what I'm talking about. What intentions do you have with Alberto?"

"None. No intentions at all. Why, did he say something to you?"

"No, he didn't say anything. But I can see how you're behaving."

"But I'm not doing anything at all, I'm not trying to get him to break up with his girlfriend, I swear it, you've misunderstood me!"

"His girlfriend? What does his girlfriend have to do with any of this, now? Dorotea, I'm not sure you've understood. I saw you following him and getting into his car with him . . . You need to leave him alone."

"But why?"

"What do you mean why? Isn't it obvious?"

"Obvious? What's obvious? That I don't deserve someone like him? You think I'm worthless, don't you?"

"No, Dorotea, it's that you're . . . What are you doing? Don't cry. You're a fantastic girl, you're sweet and you're so intelligent, it's just that you're . . . you're dead. You do understand that, don't you?"

I ran out of the store, slamming the door behind me.

I'm no one. I've never been anyone.

I got home. The bald lawyer from the fifth floor came in with me, along with his wife. While she was searching for her keys in her purse, he read aloud what was written in the

announcement posted on the front door: TOMORROW A FUMI-
GATION CAMPAIGN WILL BE CARRIED OUT THROUGHOUT THE
CITY. THE POPULACE IS THEREFORE URGED TO KEEP ALL DOORS
AND WINDOWS CLOSED AND TO TAKE IN ANY LAUNDRY THAT HAS
BEEN HUNG OUT TO DRY.

I went upstairs to the apartment. My mother wasn't home.
I opened the first drawer in her desk. I pulled out the pictures
she'd taken of me as a little girl, the ones that had been rejected
by the magazine *Lulù Bimbi*, the ones with the delayed expo-
sures and my body dissolving into the wall. I leafed through
them one by one.

Then the pictures she'd taken of me surrounded by flowers
in front of the house: in a sunny corner of the sidewalk, baby's
breath, chrysanthemums, lilies, and me. Me. Me Me Me.

I also found pictures of me, her, and Aunt Clara at Costa
Saracena. We were on the glider on the terrace: I was smiling
in my mother's arms, wearing a diaper. In another picture I was
alone, sitting in front of the TV, clutching a toy telephone. In
another one we were in Trecastagni and the sky was gray, it
must have just rained, I was wearing a pair of light-blue overalls and I had a serious expression on my face, I must have
been about four. The third picture was almost the same but
there was an opaque imprint of Aunt Clara's finger on the
right-hand corner of the photo.

I overturned the drawer. Everything fell onto the floor.

Buttons and business cards, pamphlets, more pictures, two
vials of Lexotan, a broken brooch, a piece of blue tile worn
smooth by the sea. I picked up the photos. I left the room, I
walked through the house, from the dining room to the kitchen,
to my bedroom, to the broom closet, to inside the armoires and
the walls. I left the pictures on the floor, I left them behind me,
a wake of photos, one after the other.

Me in diapers. Me smiling. Me in front of the wall, my hair

loose, me me me me me, the bread crumbs of Hop o' My Thumb to help me find my way home. Unfortunately, by the time I reached the bathtub, the bag was empty: there were no more bread crumbs.

I collapsed on my bed.

Geremia was lying on the pillow. I crushed him to my chest like a teddy bear: I'm in the cradle, I'm alive, my mother still loves me up close.

February 6 was Alberto's birthday. He blew out the candles at his apartment, I said: *"I love you."* Sara embraced him with a smile, I said: *"I love you."* He unwrapped the dive watch she had bought him, I said: *"I love you."* I slammed a fist down on the table, he furrowed his brow: "Did you hear that?"

"Hear what?"

"Is someone there?"

"There's no one, Alberto, you've got to cut this out."

I stood there, motionless, behind the table, as they cleared away the dishes. I stood there, motionless, as they turned on the TV and put in the DVD of *All About My Mother*. I stood there, motionless, until they were done watching and turned off the TV and put on their coats. I followed them to the door. I followed them into the door. Hard? Soft? Light? Dark? Weak? Strong? Alive?

They turned the key and locked me.

I heard their voices echoing down the hall; they were walking away. I heard Alberto saying: "It was something banging."

"Now, that's enough, you're losing your mind, I told you no one was there."

At home, Greta was sleeping fully dressed.

No one took off her high-heeled shoes. No one turned back the covers for her. No one closed the shutters or turned off the lights in her bedroom. No one lay down beside her, shut her eyes, gave her a kiss, held her hand.

02/08/2015: White, white, white.

The next day was Sunday. I brought a cappuccino and some pistachio pastries to his house. He seemed much better: he was walking around his apartment. Sara was ironing one of his white shirts and singing a horrendous pop song. I caressed his shoulder. Soft? Smooth?

They started fighting about me.

He said: "I've had it! Get out of my apartment!" and he was clutching his head with both hands. Sara gathered up her things from the various rooms, laughing, and left. He shut the door. I could have passed through it and gone back to be with him, but it struck me as an obscene act. My immateriality had never before struck me as so vulgar. I stayed inside the door. I stayed the door.

I thought of Anna: how long had it been since I'd seen her? I thought: *"The city of confusion is broken down: every house is shut up, that no man may come in. Isaiah 24:10."*

On February 12 Alberto missed work because he had a fever; my boss told me so. After work I bought two *cipolline* and two *accartocciate,* stuffed pastries I found in a first-rate bar on Corso Sicilia, and went to see him. He was reading a book. I got close to the page, but as always the words concealed their content from me.

I stayed to watch him brush his teeth and get into bed.

He turned out the overhead light. He lay down on the bed. I lay down next to him. You could hear traffic out on the street and, at a certain point, an ambulance. I drew closer and closer to him until there was no space between us. We were joined together like bones in a poetic articulation. The room was our articular capsule, solid and perfect. The half-open door, as insidious as a fissure in the articular cartilage, would return him to the world in a few hours. But for now Alberto was all mine. I hugged him close to me, to my whole woman-shaped void.

My legs on his, my arms on his chest. It was so sad, sad, sad to be able to touch only in one direction. To know that my touch, in spite of all the intensity that I put into it, was just air on the blind wall of his body. I'd have given anything to have even just one of the twenty-seven bones that each of my hands contained when I was alive, so that Alberto could sense my touch. I'd have given anything to get back the extraordinary enchantment of tactile perception.

I tried to squeeze him. My fingers were shipwrecked in his chest. My face pressed through to his sternum. Alberto screamed.

Horoscope for the sign of Leo (for those who died between July 23 and August 22): Mercury will form a retrograde ring in your sign. Don't try to put it on, though: no one wants to marry you.

The next day, Alberto missed work. I was so frightened that I just sat on the floor and refused to do anything, with the risk of my boss firing me. But he said nothing. Perhaps he understood. Is that possible, to understand me? After all, there was nothing to be alarmed about: it was just that his fever had returned. Of course. I stood up.

I paced back and forth in the store. I threw myself against the shelves. I ended up inside the wall, in a blind chunk of plaster. The phone rang while my boss was in the bathroom. I picked up the receiver.

"Mario? Mario, is that you? Honey?"

His wife. I emitted a husky, inarticulate sound, like the ghosts in the very worst Japanese horror movies.

"Who is this?"

Right, who am I? Who the hell am I?

A painting without a canvas. Life without atoms. Breath without flesh. Pure anachronism.

Alberto didn't come to work the next day either.

At 10:20 I left work and hurried to his apartment. He wasn't there. His clothing, with the exception of his buckskin jacket, was no longer in his armoire, and his toothbrush and bathrobe were gone from the bathroom. His suede shoes and his sneakers were missing from the shoe rack. Four pair of black socks and two pair of gray ones were missing from his drawers.

I went home.

My mother wasn't there. I set the table with the Christmas tablecloth. There were no more red plastic plates, so I got out a chipped orange china plate. I placed it in front of the chair with the teddy bear. I lit a white candle at the center of the table. I filled the bathtub. I undressed. I got in and stayed there for a week.

I didn't leave even when my mother came in to open the window to let in some fresh air. I even let a spider build its house on me, stretching from my right breast to the rim of the tub. I let two identical cockroaches run over me, and they felt only the chill of the steel.

I stopped going to work. What was the point now?

Every day I went to Alberto's uninhabited apartment but he was never there. I looked for him in every room and even in the armoire. In the broom closet. Under his bed and under the bed in the guest room. In the shower, where the soap was still caked in a corner. Not in the drawers, because when you're alive your body can't fit into such tiny spaces.

Alberto had stopped going to his apartment.

I knew that this, where the living are concerned, meant that he was missing. I knew that for the living it's imperative to return to your residence, that returning home is an integral part of the condition of living people. When children draw a house they turn the windows into eyes and the door into a mouth, so greatly do they identify their bodies with houses.

Of course, we dead—even without our material bodies—still live in our homes, but it's not important. If we fail to come home one day, if we sleep on a bus, if we spend the night out walking or sitting on the steps of a palazzo in the historic center of town, it makes no difference whatsoever. And in fact, in their drawings, dead children never transform windows into eyes. On the contrary, at the cemetery, bending over their own ruined skeletons, they play at turning their eyes into windows: they fill them with flowers, like on windowsills.

When I got home I shut myself up in my room with the phone. Every half hour I called Alberto's house, but no one ever answered. I called Sara's house too. It took a lot of nerve. No one answered. I went into my mother's bedroom. She was sleeping naked in the middle of the bed. Was it already that hot out? Or was she so depressed by this point that she just lay down without even bothering to put on her nightgown? I lay down next to her. On top of her. My legs on her legs. My lips clamped to her breast all the way down to the hard bone.

She opened her eyes. I opened my eyes. She screamed.

That night I wandered through the city. I looked for him everywhere. Alberto was nowhere to be found. Morning came. Then afternoon. Then evening. I looked for him at the cathedral with its pigeons and its shorts-clad tourists, I looked for him at the filthy bottom of the Amenano River, which reeks of carrion and vanishes underground. In the Roman aqueduct, in the overgrown, beer-can-littered paths of the Parco Gioeni, on the scalding steps of the Church of the Santissima Trinità, in the Church of Sant'Agata al Borgo. On the sidewalks of the Scogliera, and in the middle of the sea, deep down in the sea, inside the fishes. After four days I couldn't take it anymore.

I went back home. To my bedroom. To my bed.

I took Geremia out from under the pillow, I clutched him to my chest. I wept. I looked at him. I looked at him with envy. He still had palmate hands, which meant that not enough of his cells had died yet to separate his fingers. His face and his brain and his organs too were still almost undifferentiated. He wasn't yet an individual, the way I had been in life.

It's the death of billions of cells that makes us individuals. All cells die that fail to find around themselves the molecular conditions necessary to repress their own self-destruction, and it is their death that sculpts our shape.

The finished form of our hands, our eye sockets, our lips is only the result of a chain of failures, of suicides averted, of lives protracted beyond their wishes. The tip of the nose, the cavity of the nostrils, the eyes that look out onto the world and do not close are the result of a molecular constriction that has prevented a whole series of predestined deaths.

That fetus was as close to God, to heaven, to the abstract and infinite matter of the universe as anything I'd ever seen. It was a pure death impulse not yet entirely inhibited by development. That fetus was all of us before the death of our cells could carve our absolute into squalid little cookie cutters.

My breasts and my elbows, my lips—the whole map that was called Dorotea Giglio—stuck out like headstones commemorating the death of the billions of heroic cells that managed to eliminate themselves. We are a collection of all the cells that haven't managed to carry out their ancestral kamikaze mission. Our flesh, so cleanly divided between one finger and the next, is the floor plan of a forgotten necropolis.

In July of 2011 I'd never been so close to myself: I too, like all the thousands of billions of cells that died every day inside me, suddenly no longer found around myself the conditions necessary to forestall my suicide.

The next day I put Geremia into my big gray travel bag and moved to Alberto's place.

I found Anna sitting on a bench in the Parco Falcone. She told me that she'd quit her job and had lately been spending her days on that bench, praying and reciting Isaiah. She'd lost her mind. I had no idea what had become of Euridice, and I didn't care a bit. I spent all day and all night in Alberto's empty home. I never went out, I never even looked out the window. Every morning I'd get up and wander through the empty rooms.

The washing machine was empty too, and so were the medicine cabinet in the bathroom, the glasses, the bowls, the hats on the topmost shelf. I'd never noticed how much emptiness there is in objects.

One rainy Saturday, I went back to visit myself at the cemetery: even my heart, under the flies, was hollow by now. Just like Lidia's. Like my mother's and Clara's hearts when they eventually die of old age; then they'll all be the same, four collapsed hearts. Four grottoes of corroded pulp. Four old hands cupped as if to scoop up dirt. Four breakfast bowls, which at the house in Trecastagni are stitched together by a spiderweb. Four rinds of old fruit, four in four different places without ever touching. Four without blood and heat, four without anything, four empty cradles.

On February 25, 2015, I opened the refrigerator; it was empty except for a package with four strawberries inside it. The next day they were still there. The third day, same thing. Every morning, as soon as I got up, I opened the refrigerator and looked at them. The fourth day, suddenly, the strawberries were no longer themselves: they had been transformed into soft objects covered with a light-brown fur. On the fifth day there were small green worms crawling on them.

I took them into Alberto's bedroom, placed them at the center of the bed, and lay down next to them. I knew that they had something to tell me: something for me, something to understand. It was just a matter of time. If I just waited with determination, on the empty bed in the empty room in Alberto's empty home, I'd prove myself worthy of their secret. And then Alberto would come back. I put them away in the drawer, between the condoms and the aspirin.

02/26/2015: My bones are so fragile by now. Before long they're bound to break. My skull has green patches around the eyes and mouth. Soon I'll stop being organic material, I'll turn into white dust. By that day probably even the name on my headstone will have vanished entirely. And then remembering me won't be enough anymore: only radiocarbon will be able to calculate when Dorotea Giglio died, how long ago she walked the earth and spoke, read books, grew up, laughed, cried, grew older.

Hi, I'm Dorotea Giglio (1986–2011). The one who always wore a pink dress with little blue clouds. You made fun of me for that dress. You made fun of me as if it were my fault it was ugly, as if I myself were the ugliness of that dress, as if I could never be anyone in life other than the person wearing that horrendous dress. That was how I felt. I don't remember exactly what you would say, but you really hurt me, I used to cry at night. In the morning, before going to nursery school, I'd always tell my mother that I didn't want to put that dress on, but she didn't understand and she'd make me wear it, saying that she'd paid a lot of money for it. Anyway, I don't hold it against you anymore, not at all, and in fact I'd like to see you and get a drink together. I don't know if you still like playing with Play-Doh, but I sort of do. They told me that you jumped off your balcony when you were twenty. I know that we haven't talked since we were both five, but I killed myself too, so I think we'd have a lot to talk about. Ciao, hugs to you.

Today is March 1, 2015.

Soon it will be April: a peak month for both tourism and suicides. Anna, Euridice, and I all wait anxiously: the days are all beautiful because they precede a major holiday. The days are like what's behind the windows of an Advent calendar. To every new suicide we'll introduce all the others, we'll give them fried riceballs and mini-pizzas, we won't ask any of them why they killed themselves. We'll offer bracelets to the ones who, like me, slashed their wrists, because they usually want to conceal the cuts: not out of any sense of privacy or regret but rather to block a door. They're afraid they might be able to go back to where they came from.

Today is March 1, 2015.

Aboveground, spring has already arrived, but underground a black ooze is spreading, littered with dissolved scraps of my flesh and the rags of the sky-blue linen dress in which I was buried. In the Parco Falcone, surrounded by plane trees and palm trees and empty beer cans, the first geraniums have bloomed. They burst out of the soil, without shyness, everywhere. At the foot of the red, orange, and blue jungle gym with the little metal slide. Under the empty benches. Under the chairs where old men play cards. Flowers spring up everywhere: the sun bestows its rays equitably upon them all; none are outsiders. There's plenty of sunlight for all of them, and all of them will grow. Today is March 1, 2015; underground my flesh has vanished, aboveground Alberto has vanished.

You are a psychoanalyst.

An urban legend fabricated by the dead for the dead says

that across the sea there is an island of psychoanalysts who see-hear-understand the dead. Euridice told me about it. We were drinking vodka and lying by the water on the diving piers of Piazza Europa. We were looking at the water. The same waves that once triggered the nausea of seasickness now trigger the nausea of Sartre. Euridice stood up and pointed into the distance: *"There it is."*

"Actually, I remember pretty clearly that when I was alive Calabria was over there."

"You're drunk."

"Sure, of course I am. It's you, you just make up too many stories."

"No, it's true, one hundred percent true, I swear."

Deep down, we just have this great need for stories. I need them too. In fact, I've tried plenty of times to talk Euridice into letting me read her novels, but she says that would be cannibalism.

You're a psychoanalyst, and this bottle with the story of my death inside it has come to you.

Cure me; cure us.

My pain is collective, it's a field plowed by too many souls. I can furnish my pain with my thoughts, but it still remains nothing but a rental property. I can wander through its rooms, fooling myself into believing that I built all this, but it's no good, every visit will leave me with a new and terrible corner, a new darkness holed up in there. There's nothing to be done about it: I'm strictly a tourist in my pain.

My pain is my mother's pain, and the pain of her mother, who used to lock herself up with her in the guest bedroom when the sadness became too overwhelming. She would say: "Lie down with me," and they'd lie down, and she'd say: "Now let's sleep." She'd shut her eyes, and then my mother would close hers.

My pain is the stale air of the dusty house in Trecastagni and the stale air in my apartment. My pain is thirdhand, or fourth-hand. It's my mother's pain and it's her mother's mother's pain and the chain goes on without an articulation, without a break.

Cure me, cure us.

I'm writing to you even though everything seems so irremediable. I'm writing to you because in reality something has changed. I'm writing to you because my worst defect has actually always been my optimism. I was so optimistic as to hope that death would finally put an end to my suffering. I died of optimism.

The days after Alberto's disappearance went by slowly. I no longer did anything, I didn't bother anyone, I was a perfect ghost: my displacement from life was complete, perfect.

The strawberries, in the drawer, had become a shapeless gray mass, and ants were eating them. Every night, stretched out on my double bed under a poster of Ella Fitzgerald, my ears pricking up at every footstep on the apartment house stairs, I watched the TV with the sound turned off. Every morning I'd get up. I'd open the fridge, the washing machine, all the windows and armoires and the doors and the kitchen cabinets, then I'd retrace my steps and shut them all.

Ciao, my name is Dorotea Giglio (1986–2011). You don't know me. I saw you on the news, you had a resigned face and your hair was turning white. You were from Librino. Your husband had shot you out of jealousy and then he'd shot your three-year-old daughter, and after that he'd killed himself. I'd like to get to know you. Why don't you come visit me? I'm in Catania, in the center of town, I have a very comfortable place. I spend lots of time in my bedroom and in my bathroom too. It's a beautiful place, and has been since I died there. I play at doing my makeup, as if other people could still see me. I pretend to shave my legs with the razor I used to kill myself: after death, objects no longer carry the baggage of memories and symbols; they turn back into objects. At night I take a bath in the tub where I cut my wrists. I cut them open again in the same place, like buttonholes, but there's nothing inside them.

Opening myself without having a life inside threatening to leave is no more dramatic than unstitching a dress. Opening myself is a keyhole into an uninhabited room, but I go on doing it, fist clenched, razor in hand. I fall asleep that way, dreaming of emergency, and in those dreams the body is still a house: there's still someone to contain, someone to evict.

On February 28 I went to work and said to my boss: *"I'm very sorry, but I can't work here anymore. You've been very nice to me, but now I have to go."*

"Where are you going to go?"

"I don't know. I'll travel the world until I find Alberto."

"Dorotea, listen . . ."

"What is it?"

"You can't go."

"What do you mean I can't go? Why not?"

He opened the top drawer of the cash register. He pulled out a letter.

"At this point . . . Yes, maybe it's best for you to read it."

He held out his arm and handed it to me.

I opened it.

I looked at it for a long time, in terror. The rectangular shape of the opaque, unlined white sheet. The words in black ink produced by a fine-tipped .5 millimeter felt-tip pen. There was a lot of room between one line and the next, and in that space the extremities of the letters stretched exaggeratedly upward and downward, like the fins of fish abandoned on the beach. I was trembling. The letter ended an inch from the bottom of the sheet of paper. The last mark on it was an ellipsis, but that was followed by a signature.

I looked up.

"Please read it to me, I don't know how to read."

He took it. He started reading.

Dear Mario,

I'm sorry to have left the way I did, without a formal resignation. I believe I owe you an explanation. Since I started working for you, something has been happening to me that I never would have believed. It's the girl you told me about, the one who used to work for you and who killed herself. I know I must seem crazy to you, but I've seen her. I've seen her lots of times. Not only at work, at home too. For instance, when I was making dinner, sometimes she'd appear before me. I was terrified. I sensed her presence beside me in bed at night. She even stole a scarf that I'd bought for Sara. It was getting so I couldn't sleep anymore. Do you remember when I had a fever? That's when the apparitions started to proliferate. She appeared constantly. The other morning, Sara was there too, and I felt her hand touching my shoulder. I swear it. Sara never believed me. She thought I was crazy. She still thinks I'm crazy. We broke up. My life has become a nightmare. That morning, Sara was ironing and when I felt the hand on my shoulder, I screamed and scared her to death and she almost burned herself with the iron. She started yelling at me, telling me that I was out of my mind, so I had to kick her out of my apartment. In other words, you can just imagine how I felt, my life has become a true nightmare, Mario. I'm leaving Sicily, I'm going to go stay with my sister for a while. Then we'll see. But you must understand why I absolutely can't stay in Catania.

With all my best,

Alberto

I took the letter out of his hands and ripped it to pieces.

"Dorotea, I'm sorry, I . . . Try to understand . . ."

I was shaking. Was I shaking? I was crying. Was I crying?

"Where does his sister live?"

"No, Dorotea, no."

"No, what? No, what?"

I doubled over onto the floor.

He came over to me, he knelt down. Through my tearless tears I saw his elderly face, his smile. His pity.

I ran out of the store.

I didn't know what to do. I couldn't do anything. I couldn't chase after a person who would never want me. I couldn't go back to the starting point either, to when everything was damp and dark and organic and there was no loneliness yet: I had a cord that linked me to someone else.

I went home, I threw open the door to my mother's bedroom. She wasn't there. I fell to the carpet, the way I had when I was still alive and I had one of my attacks, hands on my eyes, alone with my tears and the darkness of my fingers.

I lay there, motionless, waiting for her to come back.

An hour later she came home and entered her room.

I got up, I set the table downstairs with the red Christmas tablecloth, the one with the reindeer. In the right corner you could still see the wine stain: why had no one ever removed it? Would it be there forever? I lit a white candle at the center of the table. I filled the bathtub. I got in. Stretched out in the water, surrounded by those solid walls, I felt safe. I had made up my mind. It would be quick and painless. The tub, its walls wrapped around me like hard petals, was reassuring. It was a hope. It was a uterus but without the abuse of birth.

I looked at my hands.

I only had to find a way of getting her into the tub, then it would be very easy. An instant. Push her underwater and hold on. Count to twenty the way she had counted by the River

Cassibile as the water poured into Lidia's lungs, expelling the air forever, filling her whole body.

It doesn't take much to drown. First, apnea. Then the apnea ends and the nerve centers go crazy, followed by convulsions. A final arrhythmia, then you lose consciousness, and you stop breathing. You remember, Mama, that you don't need to breathe to be together.

In 2011 the world ended: I killed myself.

The world ends every day for hundreds of people, but Anna says it will begin again soon. It's called resurrection, we're all invited, the Bible speaks clearly. *"Be not dismayed,"* says Anna.

On that day, our bodies will rise from the earth, sluggish but still self-confident, even though the self has long since been evicted. Anna takes both my hands as if they still belonged to me and says: *"Do not weep."*

Our bodies will come toward us: no need to run, there are souls for everyone. The blood will surge up imperiously, once again filling the capillaries like canals in an abandoned city. Kidneys, lungs, liver, heart tissue will all be repopulated with cells. The flesh, so worn, may seem difficult to restore: decimated abodes, from chest to thigh, to tendons, with buckled walls, usurped by plant life, but suddenly inhabited once again. The bones will join together once again in poetic articulations. On the newborn articulations, articular capsules will rise like cradles. The highways of nerves will no longer be deserted: there will always be someone going somewhere. Red blood cells will bloom again to protect these roads. Further down, the sarcophagus of the stomach will become a bridge again. The worms will slither away, the spiderwebs of secretions will flake apart. The entire amazing city that is the body, ravaged by the barbarism of enzymes, will reemerge into the light. From now on, everything will be in constant movement. Electricity will return to the brain: the city had been left in darkness for far too long. The blood will never set again: everyone will forget its collapse, the traitorous gravitational force that chased it downward, and the way the muscles hardened to follow it into the grave.

Feverishly, counting a rosary of glands, our souls will zip to the pulsating center of the city, the registry of hopes, the kennel of regrets, the dark castle haunted by illusions, the one and only: the heart.

It will be difficult to travel the rough roads of the arteries, damaged by mud, to return home to that organ that now lies in ruins, and still to respect it as it is, as we did when it was shaped like pendants hanging from the necks of lovers and balloons at the carnival. As when children drew it in the sand and adolescents drew it on school desks, on their arms, on tree bark. As when it starred in every sentimental metaphor: in those days it was lovers and pop songs, not larvae and bacteria, who implored us to "open up your heart to me." Difficult to get up there, to the summit of the body and of human dignity, crushed inside galleries of veins, now dark and gloomy and chewed up by bacteria. And once we are there, what pity we'll feel for our limping, fragile, crippled hearts. They will resemble more than ever the afflicted love that we have assigned them, the thorny, flame-engulfed heart that protrudes from Christ's chest in paintings.

Like a majestic derelict hotel, hidden behind the brambles of the sternum, the dark atria of the heart will once again be home to blood. The left ventricle, deformed by flies, will once again remember how to pump adequately. The sinus node will once again know how to speak the electric language of nerves. The arterial vessels will no longer be empty flowerpots, boarded and occupied by only the most daring roots.

The hotel will resume operation: the ramshackle beams of the ventricles will be trodden by millions of blood cells every minute. All will be reborn to the solemn notes of an organ: not the one that celebrates death at funerals, but rather the organ that keeps us alive. The lungs will have to accept the air they are offered. The muscles will have to make peace with the brain, just as the legs will take us places and the hands will touch the world. The eyelids, gummed up with dirt, will be opened like Christmas presents: best wishes for a merry resurrection.

Our sense of smell will intuit the spring, and our feet will feel the barely wet grass, but the neurons will have to cooperate. Our bodies will take their second steps, every bit as clumsy as their first steps when they were babies. And just as our parents did back then, we will kneel down smiling and praise them: "Good job!" They'll fall to a seated position: too soon for long hikes. It will be sunset: the new blood will be reflected in the sun as the sky is in the sea.

Then the transformation: we will be reunited, one inside the other.

It's hard to believe. But I can't do otherwise. I prick up my ears, but my heart is still defused. For how much longer?

Anna says: *"Don't cry."*

I wait at the cemetery, holding my body by the hand. Now without the customs barrier of the flesh, my grip goes all the way to the bone: it's called love, and it no longer hurts.

The tub was ready. The sun was setting. Some dogs were howling and others were already sleeping.

I went into my mother's room.

She was sleeping, and next to her slept Euridice, her arms wrapped around Geremia.

"What are you doing here? Get out of my house this instant, you bitch! If you even try to scare her . . ."

"I don't want to scare her."

"Then what are you doing here?"

"I've been here for years and years. Sleeping in this bed. From when you were one year old until the day you died."

"What on earth are you talking about?"

She set Geremia down on the floor. She sat down.

"It's true. I wanted to keep Greta company. She can't sleep on her own. You know, Clara is so busy with her work, and she has so many men, while Greta has always been alone. Maybe because she's used her pain to build a dam, so all the love that others give her changes course and flows away, lost. Lost, you understand? It's not that she didn't love you . . . You know it, don't you, that she loves you with all her heart? Besides, I can't seem to sleep alone either. For years, from my death until I moved here, I spent nights clinging to my body, but I could never sleep, because it's so cold on the river bottom . . ."

I couldn't believe it.

"Lidia, it's you."

"My body was found in 1987, you were one year old. They buried it, but I couldn't bring myself to stay near it: it was monstrous, swollen, ravaged, torn to shreds. Underwater I'd never noticed what bad shape I was in. I couldn't bring myself to stay near it, to sleep with it, Dorotea, and I couldn't manage to get any sleep in the house in Trecastagni either; it was too empty, and the pictures of me had all disappeared. I started to spend my nights here, I felt less lonely. And Greta liked it better too: she stopped sleepwalking. At night she no longer went out in search of me because she no longer needed to, I was here with her. I'm sorry my presence made you have nightmares. Please, forgive me."

I lay down on the right side of the bed. My mother was in the middle and Lidia was to her left.

Outside the wind was howling. The windows in the room were banging, and so were the windows in my room, and the ones in the kitchen and the bathroom.

I saw Lidia's arms reach out toward my mother and pass through her chest. I saw her whole body stretch and pass through the skin. In a few seconds the entire transparency of Lidia had fused with my mother's body. From outside they seemed like a large pulsing cell, with a heart of viscous living matter, and a large glistening membrane enveloping it.

I summoned the nerve to imitate what she had done.

I began the embrace with the arms, then the breasts, the stomach, the genitals, the thighs, the legs. At a certain point I felt an incredible heat. I felt my abstract matter deploy itself as a black light, merging, with pleasurable and violent friction, with a complicated reality of flesh and movements, of sounds, of organized actions, of gurgling machines and shattered colors, of assonances, of orchestras, of conjoined silences, of sticky figures, of curdled solids and spongy voids, of soft and porous elastic darkness, sometimes as hard as a closed door, other times as tense as a hammock. Within a few seconds there was nothing around me, because everything was within, everything was together. We were there. Stable and whole right down to the clamp of the bones, steeped in blood, intact right down to the heart. I smiled at Lidia, even though I couldn't see her. Greta's body enclosed us both.

The eyes flew open. The two eyes on my mother's face like flowers from the rock. Inside, in darkness, the other four.

Today is March 1, 2015.

I write that in 1972 Violet Trefusis died. She said that whatever you do, you must always be extreme.

That's the way I see things too. In my life I've made plenty of mistakes, but I never stopped halfway out of fear, I never hid, I never surrendered, I never shut my eyes. I remained transparent and exposed to the sun like a lens, and I caught fire.

Today is March 1, 2015.

At eight in the morning my mother received a phone call and hurried to the clinic where Aunt Clara had been admitted. A baby girl was born; her name is Dorotea. The father is unknown. In Aunt Clara's arms, and then in my mother's,

Dorotea cried like all newborns do, then she smiled. In my mother's arms, Lidia and I held her.

Outside the sun was blazing hot, and the grounds of the clinic were full of bodies. Alive or dead, damaged or intact, happy or sad or simply waiting. Bodies full of eyes. They trudged along, or they remained motionless, looking up at the windows.

From the day I died to today, I've seen so many motionless people.

Motionless on their chairs. On their unmade, sweaty beds, in dark rooms where the windows are never opened anymore. In hospitals, bandaged like mummies in sterile sheets and white bedcovers. Under the neon lights of operating rooms. In their cars, with their hands still on the steering wheels. Standing in the middle of the road, like traffic signals, or with their eyes closed on the roofs of apartment buildings, covered with pigeons. Their arms extend horizontally like someone about to leap into the void, or they form a noose around the back of the person they love while she's asleep. Their hands clutch pistols or the last of the sleeping pills. Their legs are motionless because they have nowhere to go. Their eyes are despairing: they wish that their gazes still met with a response. Each of them has his chair, her apartment building, his side of the road before the car ran him over. We cling to the last piece of the universe that recognized us: you are here, you are you, for a little while longer.

Clinging to Lidia and gathered inside Greta—curled up, scattered like oxygen, vigilant as poison—I hold my family close.

Three hours after Dorotea's birth, my mother went to the cemetery. My mother went to visit me. We're sitting on the ground by my headstone. By the last of my bones. The sun is yellow, the flowers vertical. The grass is green, the sky is starting to peel, turning red: soon it will be sunset. The branches of the pine trees around us extend into the air like nerves, and the smiles extend lazily across our faces.

When I finish writing in this diary I'm going to tear out the pages and slip them into a big glass bottle: I have a perfect one at home, we used to put the flowers that my mother photographed in it. It belonged to my grandmother, she got it on a trip to Ireland that they all took together: she, Clara, my grandparents, and Lidia. A month later Lidia would turn twenty-one, and two months later she would be dead.

Somewhere there's a photo she took in which the two others are holding hands on a gleaming lawn, smiling.

I'll go down to the sea and leave the bottle with the letter among the waves. I don't know what's written in it, but I know it will reach you. I don't know who you are—maybe my father?—but I know that I wrote it myself.

Today is March 1, 2015, and aboveground spring has arrived. Today is March 1, 2015, and my mother has brought me flowers.

ABOUT THE AUTHOR

Viola Di Grado was born in Catania, Italy, and currently lives in London. Her first novel, *70% Acrylic 30% Wool*, was the winner of the 2011 Campiello First Novel Award and a finalist for Italy's most prestigious literary prize, the Strega.